ROGUE

A BIGFOOT THRILLER

C.G. MOSLEY

SEVERED PRESS
HOBART TASMANIA

ROGUE

CHAPTER 1

October 1989

"It's already been a year," Emma Honeycutt complained as she downed the last of her Slurpee from the Dunn Sonic.

"Not quite a full year," John Milk replied as he munched on a french fry. "Next month makes a full year."

Emma rolled her eyes at him and scratched at the back of her head. "Next conversation we have with Cold, I'm asking him to reassign me," she grumbled. "This is a waste of my talent and time."

John sighed and resisted the urge to tell her she was being arrogant again. It was a trait of hers that he grew to tolerate. Emma Honeycutt was the best agent alive in her own mind. She was damn good, he had to admit, but her confidence in her abilities became a bit annoying at times.

It was a brisk night in Baker County Mississippi, and they watched the residents of Dunn go about their daily lives from the Sonic restaurant parking lot. John certainly related to Emma's circumstances. He too was frustrated and dismayed that nothing at all had happened since the events at Walker Laboratory in November of the prior year. Supposedly, Baker County was home to a large tribe of Bigfoot and rumors circulated of other cryptids lurking in the forests also. The events of the prior year had resulted in some sort of human and Bigfoot hybrid. Supposedly, the creature had escaped to the forest, but no one had seen or heard from the thing since.

"So, what are you going to be for Halloween?" Emma asked rather abruptly.

John smiled at her. "Are you serious right now?"

She looked over at him, wide-eyed. "Of course I'm serious," she answered sharply. "Why the hell would I joke about that?"

"So…you dress up for Halloween?" John tried not to laugh.

Emma looked away and watched a young boy sucking on a milkshake several cars away from them. "It's my favorite holiday. Of course I dress up."

"Well, what are you going as?" he asked, now genuinely curious.

"Haven't decided yet, John. So, I'm going to ask again, what are you going to be for Halloween?"

He shrugged. "I don't know. Wasn't really planning on going as anything. Isn't that a kid thing?"

She took a deep breath through her nose and exhaled slowly. "No, it's not just a kids' holiday," she proclaimed. "My parents never let me do it as a kid so I'm going to dress up every damn Halloween until the day I die."

John smiled. "Do what makes you happy, Honeycutt."

"Well, it would make me happy if you'd tell me what the hell you're going to be for Halloween," she persisted.

"Oh, for Christ's sake," he snapped. "I'll be a damn Sasquatch…okay?"

She narrowed her eyes at him. "Not funny. Not in this county."

"Then let me think on it."

"You've got 'til Friday and then I want an answer," she replied firmly.

"Fine! I'll give you a damn answer on Friday," he said, now exasperated with the conversation.

"So, where do you think the thing is at now?" Emma glanced up at the stars.

"The hybrid?"

She nodded.

John shrugged. "Hell, if I know," he answered. "Could be dead, I suppose."

She looked over at him, curious. "Why would you assume it's dead?"

"Well, no one has seen or heard from it in almost a year," John replied. "His sister moved away because she couldn't bear to live here anymore after what happened. He doesn't belong to the humans and it doesn't belong to the tribe of Bigfoot. He's in a strange in-between place. How can he survive that way?"

Emma shook her head and chuckled.

"What is it?" John asked.

"You keep referring to the damn thing as a *he*." She sounded somewhat disgusted.

"It is a *he*," John countered. "His name is Kurt Bledsoe and a very terrible thing happened to him."

"Correction," Emma snapped. "He used to be Kyle Bledsoe. Now it's a thing that, as you just eluded to, has no purpose. No family and nowhere to really call home anymore. The damn thing should've been destroyed."

"Well, his sister didn't think so," John said. "And neither did Sheriff Cochran."

Emma scoffed at the comment and tossed her now empty cup out of the window and into a nearby trashcan. "A lot of good it did the poor thing."

John decided to let her have the last word. "Are you ready to call it a night?"

"Yeah, sure...another day where we accomplished practically nothing," she quipped.

John cranked the car and as he prepared to shift into reverse, a blood-curdling scream pierced through the cool night air.

"What the hell?" he said, startled.

Emma does not respond; she instead scrambled from the vehicle, her gun drawn. John chased after her and they found a large woman in a nightgown, screaming frantically.

"Ma'am, calm down," John pleaded. "Tell us what is going on!"

"My son!" she screamed. "It took my son!"

"Where did it take him?" Emma asked.

The woman continued to scream but pointed toward the dark forest behind them. Without another word, Emma took off, retrieving a small flashlight from her pocket as she ran. John chased after her, doing the same. They were only in the forest a short time when they heard the cries of a young boy ahead of them.

"Stop where you are!" Emma yelled. "We are armed federal agents and you must stop now!"

The boy screamed at them for help, but he seemed to be getting further away.

"We're losing them," John said as he pulled alongside Emma.

"I'm not stopping." Determination fired her statement.

As they continued, the young boy's cries became more and more distant until finally, they could no longer hear him at all.

Emma continued to run until her body could no longer carry her forward. She collapsed onto her hands and knees, panting furiously.

"We lost them," John panted beside her.

"We've got to keep going," she said. "Whoever that was can't get away with this."

"You know damn well what it was," John snapped. "That wasn't a man…no man can run that fast!"

Emma shook her head. "It's going to kill that boy."

John nodded but said nothing.

"We're just going to let it happen?" Emma asked, still breathing heavily.

"Come on," John said, grabbing her shoulder. "Let's go back to the car and call the sheriff. We'll come up with a plan."

They walked briskly back to the car and on the way, Emma stepped on something that crunched under her feet. She stopped, shining her light on the ground and illuminating a half-empty milkshake cup. It belonged to the boy she'd been watching while in the car.

When they finally returned to the parking lot, the boy's distraught mother was seated at a picnic table surrounded by Sonic employees.

"Did you find him?" she asked through tears.

Emma shook her head. "No, ma'am, not yet," she said sympathetically. "But we will. We're going to get the local sheriff's department to assist in the search."

"I called the sheriff," the manager of Sonic told her. "He should be here any minute."

John leaned near the woman. "Ma'am, can you give us a description of who took your son?"

The woman looked at him, bewildered. "It wasn't a man!" she exclaimed. "It was one of those things from the forest!"

John glanced over at Emma to see she was already staring at him, her gaze piercing.

"Tell me your son's name, his age, and what he was wearing," John asked, trying to act as if the woman's revelation hadn't swayed him.

The woman continued to sob, and a Sonic employee offered her a cup of water. She finally managed to regain her composure enough to answer his questions. John learned the boy's name was Lucas Hurst. He was eight years old and wearing a pair of denim shorts and a white shirt with red stripes. His mother had sent him out of the car to dispose of their trash when he was abruptly taken. She'd just barely caught a glimpse of the thing that took him but was certain it was one of the wood apes that were known to inhabit the forests of Baker County.

Strobing blue lights pulled John and Emma's attention away from the woman. Sheriff Ray Cochran brought the large patrol car to a screeching stop near them and the man's large frame exited the vehicle and jogged toward them.

"Was it one of them?" he asked.

John nodded.

"Yeah, it was one of those sons of bitches," Emma growled. "If I didn't know better, I'd say it's the one you helped free."

"No," Sheriff Cochran said. "It wasn't Kurt. There's no way."

"Sheriff, please find my boy!" the woman wailed in agony.

"We'll find him, Mary," he replied, seemingly aware of who the woman was.

A deputy arrived and Cochran had him see to the woman. Once he had John and Emma out of earshot, he asked, "Which way did the thing take him?"

John pointed to where they went into the forest.

"We chased him as far as we could but finally lost track," Emma said bitterly.

"I know a road that goes through the forest in the direction you say they went." The sheriff walked back toward his vehicle. "Get in the car," he told them. "Maybe we'll get lucky and cut them off."

Cochran sped along the curvy dark roads until they finally reached a very secluded spot in the heart of the forest. He pulled the car off the road, the blue lights still strobing.

"I say we spread out," the sheriff suggested. "I'll go straight ahead and you two go parallel to me further out."

"Sounds like a plan," John said as he readied his weapon.

"Fire a shot in the air if you see anything," Emma said, and she quickly ran away into the darkness.

John shined his light in all directions as he went, and he began to shout the boy's name.

"Lucas! Lucas, can you hear me?"

The only reply he received was the own echo of his words returning to him. He traveled deep into the woods, so far that he was beginning to think it was time to turn back. His light scanned the environment ahead of him and suddenly he caught a glimpse of something odd. He moved the light carefully back to what caught his gaze, and he cringed as it illuminated what he'd feared he'd seen before. Bright red blood.

John fired a shot into the air to let the sheriff and Emma know he'd found something. As he waited, he began to follow the trail of blood in hopes he'd find something positive that would lead to a happy ending for young Lucas Hurst. His hopes were dashed soon as he came across a boy's sneaker. It was stained in blood.

John held a hand over his mouth as he crouched to examine the shoe. He clearly saw it had once been white but was now soaked almost entirely red. It wasn't a good sign and his heart sank.

"John!" Sheriff Cochran called out as he approached.

"Over here," he replied, still crouching over the shoe.

The sheriff drew closer to him and John heard him gasp.

"Yeah, not good," he said in response.

"No, it's not the shoe," Cochran said, his voice trembling a bit.

John turned and shined his light in the direction where Sheriff Cochran was standing. On the ground in front of his boots lay a severed arm—a boy's arm ripped away just above the elbow.

CHAPTER 2

"So, what is it exactly that you'd have me do?" Sheriff Cochran asked tiredly.

"Your job," Emma replied, frustration in her tone.

John rubbed his eyes and took a gulp of coffee. It was almost two o'clock in the morning and he desperately wanted to sleep. "Sheriff, we just think that the sooner you get a search party in those woods, the better. The boy is most likely dead, true enough, but we need to act fast if we're gonna find whoever is responsible."

"And I told you," Cochran responded, staring at the two of them sharply. "I'll get every man I can get in those woods first thing in the morning.

Cochran closed his eyes, looked away, and sighed.

"And you're here cowering in your office," Emma continued. "Cowering because you're afraid you don't have enough men to deal with that..." she paused as she contemplated the right word. "That *thing*," she said finally. "You're afraid and it's pretty damn obvious."

"Honeycutt, that's enough," John said, stepping forward and gesturing at her with his hand.

Sheriff Cochran rubbed at the back of his neck and grumbled something under his breath. "Fine, damnit," he said, sounding defeated. "Me and my deputies will go out there tonight and see if we can track it."

Lightning flashed from beyond the window and thunder rumbled soon after.

"Maybe he's right," John said, glancing over at Emma. "A storm is rolling in."

"The one that took that boy, it's not who you think it is," the sheriff said abruptly. "It's not Kurt Bledsoe."

Emma stepped forward, the cigarette dangling from her mouth. "Oh yeah? How can you be so sure?"

"Because I've been around him in his current…state," Cochran explained. "He wouldn't do this. There is too much of his human side still in there."

Emma rolled her eyes and took a long drag off her cigarette. She exhaled the smoke through her nose. "Sheriff, please stop," she muttered. "You're gonna make me cry here."

Sheriff Cochran snorted and then stomped toward a hook hanging on a nearby wall where his rain gear hung. "I'm headed back over there to look for this thing, Ms. Honeycutt," he growled. "You stay in here where it's nice and dry, okay?"

Emma smiled at him. "Yeah, I think I'll hang around and question the witness a little bit more," she replied arrogantly.

John sighed and shook his head. "Sheriff, I'm going with you," he said. "Do you have an extra poncho or something."

Sheriff Cochran nodded. "Got one in the trunk of my car," he answered. "Not going to turn down your help."

The two men trudged toward the glass door as another streak of lightning illuminated the parking lot outside.

"You boys try not to catch a cold," Emma called out after them. "Catch whatever the hell took that boy instead."

Sheriff Cochran seemed to ignore her and barged out into the windy night. John glared at her and paused at the door. "Honeycutt, when you finish questioning Mrs. Hurst, the car is out here if you'd like to come join us." He tossed her the keys.

She caught them and shoved them into her coat pocket in one fluid motion. "Thanks, Milk," she said with a smirk. "Sure, I'll be right over. Be watching for me."

***

"Why is she like that?" Sheriff Cochran asked as he piloted the boxy patrol car along the rural roads of Baker County.

John chuckled. "Don't take it so personally," he said. "You should be used to how she is by now."

Cochran glanced over at him. "You are?"

John's eyes widened slightly, and he turned his attention to the windshield in front of him. "Well...I suppose if I'm honest, that's a big N-O."

"So how the hell do you deal with it?"

"She's actually really good at her job," John explained. "What she said about questioning Mrs. Hurst some more...she's not bullshitting. She's gonna run that poor woman through the ringer to make damn sure there isn't another piece of information she can pry out of her to point us in the right direction."

"So, you're saying she doesn't believe it was a wood ape?"

"I'm saying she's open to all possibilities, no matter how unbelievable," John replied. "That's one of the things that makes her so good."

The big car rumbled along for several more miles until finally they reached the point where they'd searched for Lucas Hurst hours earlier. There were already other patrol cars parked there, blue lights strobing in all directions. As Cochran pulled the car to a stop, the rain began to fall.

"Perfect," he grumbled as he exited the vehicle.

John pulled the poncho on over his head and then grabbed a Baker County Sheriff's Department ball cap off the back seat in hopes it would at the very least help keep the rain out of his face.

"Alright, fellas," the sheriff said as he approached the four deputies. "I know it's late and I know the weather isn't great," he added as thunder rumbled overhead. "But after careful consideration, I think it best we get out there and comb through these woods one more time to see if we can find that boy. We'll have help in the morning but until the sun rises, we're on our own. Keep your gun drawn, but if you have to use it, you better know damn well what you're shooting at."

The deputies looked at each other and John could see a bit of uneasiness in their faces.

"If we find that boy, we're gonna call it a night. He is most likely dead, so at this point, I don't think it would be accurate to call this a search and rescue. Having said that, I just know if it was my kid, I wouldn't want him left out here all night in weather like this and it wouldn't matter if he was alive or dead. Let's find Lucas and give the mother some closure."

A skinny deputy with horn-rimmed glasses stepped forward. He had dark hair, almost shoulder-length, and it was already beginning to stick his neck from all the rain. "Sheriff, are you saying if we see this thing that took the boy...we're supposed to kill it?"

Cochran sighed and glanced over at John. "Billy, keep in mind, we're not completely certain who or what took the boy," he answered.

"Having said that, if you find a wood ape out there, yes, you've got authorization to shoot to kill."

Deputy Billy Stratton swallowed so hard John could see his Adam's apple bob as he did so. He was clearly nervous.

"Alright, let's get on with it," Cochran barked, water now dripping steadily from the brim of his hat. "If you find anything, call it out over the radio immediately...that clear?"

The deputies all nodded in unison and began to move away to their respective search zones.

"Where should I go?" John asked.

The sheriff looked him up and down and shrugged. "You don't know these woods, Milk. It would probably be best if you stay with me."

John shook his head. "No, you're already very undermanned for this job as it is. I'm going to carry my weight. I can find my way back to the road."

Cochran nodded. "Alright then," he said, and then he glanced further up the road. "I suppose you could go about a hundred yards that way and start making your way through the forest."

"That's too far out," he answered and then glanced over his shoulder at the forest on the opposite side of the road. "Why isn't anyone focusing any attention over there?"

"We were going to do that once we've combed this side," the sheriff answered. "If you want to get a head start, knock yourself out."

There was another flash of lightning and the rain poured harder. "I think that's exactly what I'm going to do," John said as he began to walk away.

"Fire your gun if you find anything," Cochran called after him. "I'll come running."

"Will do," John answered.

Seconds later, he disappeared within the shadows of the forest.

***

The poncho turned out to be of minimal use to John as the torrential downpour hounded him relentlessly. That, however, wasn't the worst of it. What he hadn't prepared for was the matter of his footwear being inadequate for the muddy conditions he now found himself in. What he needed was rain boots but unfortunately what he was wearing instead were black dress shoes.

Damn things are ruined, he thought sourly. As he wandered deeper into the forest, his mind seemed to stay focused on his shoes and where he'd be able to find new ones the next day. He'd tried using his flashlight but soon decided his chances of finding the wood ape would be much better if he kept it off. His eyes adjusted quickly to the dark environment and the lightning flashes every minute or so were a huge help for visibility.

John kept his gun firmly in his grip and his eyes scanned all directions in front of him as he continued to keep his concentration on his shoes. Suddenly, without any real understanding of why, he began to feel uneasy. At first, John had a hard time understanding what had brought on the feeling, but it clearly got worse with every step that he took. He felt as if someone, or something, was watching him. With every breath he took, it felt like whatever it was, it was getting closer to him. He abruptly whipped around to look behind him just as a flash of lightning ripped across the sky overhead. John blinked as he saw what he thought was a shadow moving quickly across the forest floor, obviously trying to avoid being seen.

Am I seeing things?

John kept his eyes on the area where he'd seen the shadow until another flash of lightning occurred. He saw nothing. A strong gust of wind tore through the forest, whipping up rain-soaked leaves as it did so. John instinctively returned his attention to where he'd been heading and as he began to move forward again, the uneasy feeling returned. Without hesitation, he whipped his head around again to look behind him. This time, he clearly saw it as the lightning flashed.

The wood ape was nearly eight feet in height, with hair so dark it was almost black. John couldn't tell if the beast's hair was truly that dark, or it was the raining making it appear so. He couldn't make out any facial features at all but what he could clearly see was the thing moving toward him.

"Stop right there!" John shouted as forcefully as he could. "I mean it, stop or I'll shoot you!"

The thought occurred to him that most likely the creature had no idea what he was saying. He wondered if it even knew what a gun was. If it didn't, then it would most certainly not see it as a reason to stop advancing toward him.

John kept the barrel of his gun trained on the creature as it continued to lumber toward him. He walked backward but was quickly losing ground to the approaching wood ape. It soon became very apparent that the beast wasn't going to stop. Just as John squeezed the trigger to stop it in its tracks, his heel caught a rock and he toppled backward, the shot firing innocently into the air. His bottom splashed into the squishy muck and his shoes were unable to grip the soft earth when he attempted to get up.

Before he even knew what was occurring, the wood ape reached forward and grabbed him by the ankle. It was at this point John realized he'd lost his weapon in the thick mud around him. The beast kept moving forward and dragged John behind it.

"Stop it!" he yelled while he thrashed violently to break free of its grasp.

John dug his fingers into the earth as hard as he could, a frantic yet futile attempt to stop the creature's progress. The result of his efforts only produced long, thin trails where his fingers raked through the mud. The grip around his ankle was tight and felt like a vise. There was no point in trying to pry his leg free; he simply wasn't strong enough.

He began to consider the possibilities ahead of him. Was he about to be bludgeoned to death? Would he be eaten alive? Could the wood ape be taking him to its den where the final thing he'd see would be the remains of young Lucas Hurst? John tried to push the thoughts aside.

Think, damnit…

Suddenly, without any warning, the wood ape stopped and released its grip.

John wasted no time in trying to crawl away. He frantically tried to get to his feet again, but his haste worked against him. Ultimately, he began to crawl as quickly as he could. All he could think about was putting as much distance between he and the wood ape as humanly possible. John soon stopped his efforts as a realization occurred to him. He glanced over his shoulder to see that the wood ape wasn't pursuing him. It had remained in the same spot and John could see the hulking beast breathing deeply, its shoulders rising and falling slowly.

Lightning flashed again and illuminated John's surroundings just long enough for him to get a quick look at the wood ape. The creature was staring at him and its eyes were bright and green. There was something on the ground behind it and John cringed when he realized what it was. The woods were dark again, but he could just make out the silhouette of the creature and the object mere feet behind it. John, suddenly feeling that the beast wasn't interested in hurting him, began to crawl toward the object on the ground. When he got within ten feet of it, the wood ape bolted. John could hear it crashing through the forest, seemingly eager to get as far away from him as possible.

He could hear someone calling out to him from somewhere behind him. He almost answered them but as he realized what he was looking at, a lump rose in his throat that prevented him from responding. Lightning flashed again and his worst suspicion became reality.

"Son of a bitch," Sheriff Cochran said somberly just as he stopped behind John. "You found him."

CHAPTER 3

"Here, drink this," Emma said as she shoved a steaming Styrofoam cup in John's face.

He waved her off.

"I'll pass," he said, sounding defeated. "What I need right now is sleep."

They were back in the sheriff's station—specifically the breakroom—and sunrise was roughly two hours away. Emma leaned against the counter that expanded across the entire back wall of the room. She pulled the cup of coffee back and took a drink for herself.

"Take the car back to the apartment and get some sleep. If anything further is needed from you, I'll get with you later."

John felt that he should argue but as he glanced down at his now mud-caked pants and shoes, he knew he had no real good case to do so. Emma seemed hesitant to believe his wild tale of the wood ape dragging him by the leg at first. She tried to suggest that maybe he'd bumped his head and since there had been so much talk about the creature prior to his encounter, perhaps he'd imagined it, or maybe even dreamed it when he'd been temporarily knocked out. He hadn't been knocked out, of course, and it took him raising his voice at her to finally make Emma believe him. Reluctantly, he rose to his feet and prepared to leave.

"You're right," he said, stifling off a yawn. "I'll get some shut-eye for a few hours and I'll come back, bright-eyed and bushy-tailed."

"No rush." She walked over to him and gently grabbed his arm, tugging him toward the door.

"Damn, I'm not an invalid," he grumbled.

"I know that," she said. "But if I don't start ushering you to the door right now, you'll change your mind and I'll have to spend another hour trying to convince you all over again."

As they moved down the hallway, John caught a glimpse of Mrs. Hurst through the blinds in an office window. There was a man in a suit with her. John guessed he was probably a preacher because he appeared to be praying with her. The woman was still sobbing, and she looked much more exhausted than him. He couldn't imagine the hell she was going through.

"Poor woman," Emma said. "She was so hopeful when I was speaking with her after you guys left. She said she believed God was going to protect her son and get him home. I wonder how she feels about God now."

"Well, she's currently in there praying to him, so there's that," John replied. "Besides, God didn't do this."

Emma rolled her eyes. She did that a lot. "Well, he sure as hell let it happen."

John shook his head and sighed. "The thing that did that to Lucas didn't have anything to do with God. It was evil."

They finally reached the exit and, once outside, Emma walked with him to the car.

"Are you going to be alright without the ride?" he asked as he took the keys from her.

"Are you kidding? Sheriff Cochran is my own personal chauffeur. He does whatever I ask him to do. You know that."

John thought back to the brief conversation he and the sheriff had had about Emma on the drive to look for Lucas. He smiled. "You should go a little easier on that guy."

"I'll think about it," she quipped.

"You do that," he replied, opening the door.

Emma stared at him very hard and he could tell she wanted to ask him something but was contemplating how to do it—or whether she should do it at all.

He paused and looked at her. "Something on your mind, Honeycutt?"

She sighed and bit her lip. Her eyes looked up at the moon in the sky, partially hidden by the remnants of storm clouds that had rolled through a short time earlier.

"It's nothing," she muttered. "I'm sure things will make a lot more sense once you've had some rest and we can discuss it then."

He raised an eyebrow and then proceeded to take his dirty coat off. "Discuss *what* exactly?" he asked, tossing the coat onto the passenger seat.

She smiled and shook her head. "No, it can wait. It *should* wait."

John glared at her and then shut the car door. "I'm not leaving until you spit it out."

Emma crossed her arms and closed her eyes. "Damn, I've got to learn to keep my mouth shut."

"Don't see that happening any time soon, now spit it out."

"Fine," she said quickly. "The wood ape."

"What about it?"

"You really think it was Kurt Bledsoe?"

He pinched the bridge of his nose and shut his eyes, trying his best to keep his cool. "Really? I've got to explain this all over to you again?"

"No!" she snapped. "You don't. Go home, get some rest. We can talk about it later."

"Sure, and when we do, my story will be exactly the same," he answered. "I know what the hell I saw. The damn thing wasn't trying to hurt me. It was trying to show me the kid's body."

She pushed a lock of blonde hair out of her face and took a deep breath. "And you are positive that the thing had green eyes?"

"Yes, I'm positive," he answered firmly. "The eyes appeared human. It's just the way Cochran described them in the report you yourself completed after the incident at Walker Laboratory last year."

"Alright," Emma said, holding her hands up. "If that's what you say you saw then...I guess I believe you."

John shook his head and opened the car door. "Well, that's mighty gracious of you," he growled as he got behind the wheel. He slammed the door shut and then sped out of the parking lot.

Emma watched as the taillights on the car disappeared into the darkness.

We'll see how you feel after you sleep it off, she thought defiantly.

***

"Rise and shine," Sheriff Cochran said. He playfully knocked Emma's propped legs off the desk in front of her. The chair she was sitting in squeaked in protest as her entire body shifted forward.

"What the hell?" she snapped, suddenly awake and annoyed.

"If you were gonna do this, why didn't you just go with Milk?" he asked.

The sheriff plopped a ceramic mug of coffee in front of her. It slammed harder against the wooden desk than he intended and some of the dark liquid sloshed out. Emma eyed the steaming mug and then went for it.

"What time is it?"

Cochran glanced at his watch. "Almost two o'clock. You seemed to have fallen asleep while filling out that paperwork."

"Yeah," she replied, yawning. "I thought I could hold out until Milk got back. Apparently, I was wrong."

The sheriff noticed a file on her desk with the words WATKINS LABORATORY written on the tab. "What the hell is this?" he grumbled, reaching for the file.

Emma slammed her down on top of it. "Not for your eyes, Sheriff," she said. "I'm sorry."

He shot her an icy stare. "Not for my eyes, huh? Honeycutt, I don't know if you remember this or not, but I *lived* that shit and saw it with my own eyes."

Emma looked down at her hand on top of the file and chewed at her lip. She then gradually moved her gaze up to meet Cochran's. He was right. He knew pretty much everything in that file. The real reason she'd pulled it in the first place was to let John look at the pictures and other documents related to Kurt Bledsoe. She wanted to discuss the matter with him again when he was rested, and this time, she'd have the pictures.

"Alright," she said after contemplating the matter for a few seconds. "I suppose you're right." She pulled her hand away and the folder off the desk.

He thumbed through the documents and then momentarily stopped on a photograph. "Look at his eyes," he said, holding it up.

Emma looked at the image of the wood ape and then to the brilliantly green eyes. "Yes, I've heard a lot about those eyes," she said.

"There isn't another creature around here with eyes like this," he said. "Reason being, this particular wood ape is part human. Milk said the one that grabbed him last night had these eyes and there is no doubt in my mind that it was Kurt Bledsoe."

She sighed and took another gulp of coffee. "Okay, so here is what I don't understand. If you guys are so hell-bent on that wood ape being good-hearted, part-human, Kurt Bledsoe, then why the hell didn't he intervene and save Lucas Hurst's life?"

Cochran flipped through a few more documents and shook his head. "I can't answer that," he said. "Maybe he tried and was too late."

"Or maybe sweet little Kurt Bledsoe was preparing to make a meal of Milk but was spooked when you showed up suddenly. Maybe Lucas didn't fill his belly—did you ever consider that?"

He gave her a sour look and then tossed the file back onto the desk. Some of the paper inside it came out and spread across the wooden surface. "You are one stubborn-ass woman, you know that?"

He walked away and Emma took the opportunity to flip him off when his back was turned.

Sheriff Cochran made his way further into the building until he reached his office. No sooner did he sit down at his desk did his phone ring. He glanced over at it and gave it the same sour look he'd just shot Emma. The phone was apparently unfazed because it continued to ring. He cursed under his breath and snatched it up.

"Yes, Shelly?" he grumbled.

"Sheriff, there's a man up here to see you," she answered.

"What does he want?"

"He says he has some information about the incident last night with the Hurst boy."

Cochran suddenly perked up. "I'll be right there," he said, slamming the phone down.

As he made his way back up the hallway, he paused and motioned for Emma to follow him when he reached her. She said nothing but got up and followed him the rest of the way. Once they reached the lobby, they met a man dressed in overalls, a white T-shirt, and a red baseball cap waiting for them. He appeared anxious and desperate to speak to someone in authority as quickly as possible.

"Sheriff Cochran," the man said, holding out his hand. "My name's Clifford Lowe, but everyone calls me Cliff."

Cochran nodded and shook his hand firmly. "Nice to meet you, Cliff," he replied with a smile. "This young lady here beside me is Emma Honeycutt. She's an agent with the federal government. Shelly here said you had some information regarding the incident last night?"

Cliff seemed to ignore the question and eyed Emma curiously. "Sheriff, is she F.B.I.?"

Cochran glanced at her and chuckled. "No, not at all," he murmured. "We could tell you which specific department she works for, but then we'd have to kill you."

Cliff's eyes widened but stayed on Emma. She stared right back at him and forced a smile.

The sheriff's gaze moved back and forth between them for a few awkward beats before he finally said, "So, how about that information you've got for us, Cliff?"

Cliff finally broke eye contact with Emma and glanced over at him. "Oh, yes," he muttered, seemingly coming out of a trance. "The wood ape that took the boy...I know exactly which one it was."

Cochran and Emma eyed him curiously.

"Excuse me?" she said. "You say you know specifically which wood ape killed Lucas Hurst?"

He nodded. "That's right, ma'am."

The sheriff took a deep breath. *It appears we've got a whacko here...*

"Cliff, uh, do you care to elaborate a little bit?"

"Sure can," he replied. "That same wood ape attacked me about four years ago. I've been tracking the son of a bitch ever since."

Cochran and Emma looked at each other simultaneously.

"Well, then," the sheriff said, suddenly intrigued. "I think we need to go back to my office and discuss this over some coffee and donuts. What do you say, Cliff?"

Cliff smiled. "Do you have any chocolate?"

Cochran smiled back. "I got chocolate, glazed, jelly-filled...whatever you want Cliff. Come on back and make yourself comfortable."

CHAPTER 4

Sheriff Ray Cochran's office was large enough to easily accommodate the three of them for a nice, long discussion regarding what Cliff Lowe knew about the abduction of Lucas Hurst. He seemed so excited to talk he could barely contain himself, and once he began speaking, it seemed he'd never stop. He told the sheriff and Emma a wild tale about an encounter he'd had four years prior in Sanderson Swamp.

"So, you're saying this particular creature is a rogue and has been banished from the rest of its tribe?" Emma asked, her words oozing skepticism.

"That's exactly what I'm saying," Lowe replied, nodding his head enthusiastically. "That thing is evil, so evil that its own kind doesn't even want it around them anymore. Now that it's out there and on its own, it must scrounge for food wherever it can get it. It seems that in recent years, it's taken an interest in humans as a potential food source. To my knowledge, I'm the first one it went after."

Cochran scratched at the stubble on his chin. It had been a couple of days since he'd shaved. "I still don't understand how you're so sure this is the same creature that attacked you. Seems to me you're making a lot of assumptions here."

"Did it have one eye?" Cliff asked sharply.

Cochran glanced over at Emma. She looked back at him and shifted uneasily in her chair.

"Mrs. Hurst did make mention of the fact that she thought, in her words, 'the thing had a messed-up eye,'" Emma answered reluctantly.

Cliff smiled as he watched the surprised looks grow on both their faces. "You know how that eye got messed up?" he asked.

"No," Cochran replied. "But I guess you're gonna tell me."

"It's like that because I had to shove a knife in its eye to make it let me go," he said proudly. "I was trying to kill it, but in case you weren't aware, they are damn hard to kill."

The sheriff's jaw tightened as he thought back to the encounters he'd had with the beasts in Walker Laboratory. It was true; they were indeed hard to kill.

"Alright," he said, momentarily pushing those thoughts aside. "I believe you. It's the same wood ape. Now, do you have any additional information that can help us find the damn thing?"

Cliff looked at him and seemed briefly confused by the question. "Well, I suppose I could show you where it lives," he said after thinking a moment.

Emma sat up straight. "Wait, you know where it lives?" she asked, awestruck.

Cliff looked at her and nodded.

Sheriff Cochran walked closer to him and crossed his arms. He stood over Cliff and looked down at him. "How could you possibly know that?" he asked, a bit skeptical.

"After what happened to be in '85, I've sort of become obsessed with finding the thing," he replied rather sheepishly. "Actually, I prefer to call it a hobby…or maybe passion is a better word."

"Can you take us to it?" Emma asked.

"Of course I can. But I shouldn't."

Cochran rubbed at the back of his neck. He was tired and getting a little cranky.

"And why exactly *shouldn't* you?" he said, a bit of annoyance in his tone.

Cliff opened his mouth to answer, but then quickly closed it as he contemplated what to say. "Well, how many men are you bringing?"

"How many *should* I bring?"

"How many you got?"

"Get to the point, Mr. Lowe," Emma snapped.

The directness of her tone startled him. "I—I just think you should bring all the men you can," he stammered. "It moves really fast and it's real strong. There's not a lot of margin for error."

"I'll take my chances," the sheriff said. "How soon can you show us where it lives?"

"Today," Cliff answered. "But you're not gonna find it there until the early morning hours."

"And why is that?" Emma asked.

"Because it won't be home until then," he replied. "It leaves around five in the afternoon every day to forage for food. It doesn't return 'til almost sunrise most of the time. By the time you got your men together and made the drive over there, it'd be too late today."

Emma considered what he'd said and pulled a Jupiter cigarette from the pack she'd had in her coat pocket while she did so.

"How soon can you get your men ready to go and catch this thing in the woods where it lives?" she asked, the cigarette now dangling from her mouth. She retrieved a lighter from the same coat pocket and lit it.

"I can have them all there just before sunrise," Cochran answered, trying to make sure he gave his men as much time to rest as possible.

Emma nodded and blew smoke from her mouth. "I think that's going to be our best move," she said, and then she turned to look at Cliff. "Mr. Lowe, where would be the best place for us to meet tomorrow morning so you can tell us where this thing's den is located?"

"Come to my house," he answered. "There's a trail that leads into the woods behind my house. It's a short hike and I'm the only one that knows the path, so I'll have to go with you."

Sheriff Cochran glanced over at her and could tell immediately she didn't like the idea of Cliff coming along with them. He could see Emma mulling it over in her head and he quickly decided to keep the conversation moving along so she wouldn't begin insisting that Cliff remain in his home.

"Mr. Lowe, I'm gonna need your address," he said, snatching a yellow legal pad off his desk.

Cliff told him and after a few more minutes of chit chat, the three of them shook hands, and Cliff Lowe exited the building.

"He shouldn't go with us," Emma said as soon as he was gone.

Sheriff Cochran sighed. "Agent Honeycutt, where are you from?"

She stared at him blankly. "I'm not sure what that has to do with anything but I'm from Sacramento."

"Ah," he replied. "Thought so."

Her brow furrowed. "And what exactly do you mean by that?"

"Well, it's clear you have spent very little time in the woods."

The look on her face gave away that he was right. "I'm still waiting to hear what this has to do with anything," she said, sounding annoyed.

He chuckled. "If you spent any significant time out there, you'd know that searching for a Bigfoot den will be like looking for a needle in a haystack."

"He can draw us a map," she shot back.

Cochran shook his head. "It's not that simple. This is dense forest and I don't care if he's a professional cartographer, if we're going to find this thing quickly, we'll need his help."

Emma finished her cigarette and extinguished the butt on Cochran's desk. He couldn't stand it when she did that. "Fine," she said. "But he's a civilian and he's going to be your responsibility, not ours."

He smiled and nodded, knowing full well that was going to be her response. "You better go check on Agent Milk," he said. "Someone needs to let him know about this new development."

She headed for the door. "I'll handle it. You and your men meet us at Mr. Lowe's house at 4:30 a.m. sharp."

"We will be there," he replied. "Dress appropriately."

She rolled her eyes and left the station.

***

John Milk was awake and had just gotten out of the shower when he heard the doorbell. With a towel wrapped around his waist, he hurried to the door and opened it to find Emma standing there.

"Oh, for God's sake, go put on some clothes," she muttered as she barged in past him.

He sighed and closed the door. "I assume there's a good reason you just showed up here unannounced?"

"I called but you didn't answer," she said. She went into the kitchen, grabbed a glass, and filled it with water from the kitchen sink.

"I've got bottled water in the fridge," John said.

"Water is water," she said after taking a gulp from the glass. "That'll never *really* catch on."

He smiled and crossed his arms. They were both standing in the kitchen. "I didn't answer because I was in the shower. What's up?"

"I'm about to head over to get some sleep myself," she said after she finished the water. She placed the glass in the sink behind her. "We got a real good lead on where to find the wood ape."

John's eyes widened. "Seriously?"

She nodded. "A man came into the station earlier. He said he's had his own close encounter with our wood ape back in 1985."

"1985? Well then, that's before—"

"Before the events that transpired with Kurt Bledsoe," she interrupted. "Yeah, I know."

He smiled at her, a wide toothy grin.

"Go to hell," she grumbled. "Just because he's not *the* wood ape that killed Lucas Hurst doesn't mean he's not dangerous."

"That may still be the case, but right now, our focus isn't with him."

She looked him up and down again. "No, right now, your focus should be on getting dressed. I'll meet you at the car at 4:00 a.m."

John shook his head as she moved briskly out the door. The reality was that Sheriff Cochran wasn't the only one wondering why she was the way she was.

CHAPTER 5

Emma Honeycutt woke up in a cold sweat. She didn't have many nightmares, but what she'd just experienced was exactly that. She dreamt that the vicious wood ape that had once been Kurt Bledsoe had grabbed her in the forest. The beast dragged her deeper into a dark cave and then ripped her apart, tearing into her flesh while she was still alive. She could see the rage in his bright green eyes. The dream terrified her to the point that she sat straight up in the bed. She was panting hard and shaking.

Get a grip, Emma, she thought.

She glanced over at the clock on the nightstand next to the bed. It was almost 3:00 a.m.

"Damnit," she grumbled as she rubbed the cobwebs from her eyes.

Her alarm had been set for 3:30 so as it was, there was no time to really go back to sleep. Reluctantly, she trudged out of bed and made her way to the bathroom. After showering, she put on jeans and a button-up shirt that she didn't mind getting dirty. The sheriff had told her to "dress appropriately" and though she'd never admit it to him, she knew he was more knowledgeable about the forest and what was in it than her. It pained her to accept, but she knew he was right about her experience in the forest. Hers was next to zilch.

Once she was fully dressed and her blonde hair placed in a ponytail, Emma stepped into the cool darkness of Dunn, Mississippi. She was on an upper-level apartment directly across from where John stayed. She glanced down from the balcony and could see the interior light on in the car. John was always punctual and on time. She was too. It was probably the only thing they had in common.

"Wow, I didn't even know you owned jeans," he said as she approached the car.

Emma looked him up and down and was surprised to see he was still wearing his usual black suit and tie. "You should've talked with the sheriff before you made a decision on what to wear this morning."

"I'm fine with what I've got on," he said. "I don't have any plans of rolling around on the ground with this thing."

She let it go and got in the car. "Look, we've both got to be on the same page when we meet up with the sheriff," she said as he climbed in behind the wheel.

"Okay," he said, unsure of her meaning.

"We've got to make it very clear that we are in charge of this operation."

"That's always been the case," John said, still confused. "Something bothering you?"

She glanced over at him as he pulled the car out of the lot. There was a moment she considered telling him about her nightmare but ultimately decided to keep it to herself. "No, nothing bothering me," she said. "I've just noticed you two becoming a little chummy here lately and I don't want you to forget that we've been put here by Mr. Cold to do a job. Sheriff Cochran doesn't get the final say on anything related to the wood apes or any other cryptids we encounter in this county."

"Agreed. I've got your back—you know that."

She smiled and his response seemed to help. "I know, and I've got yours."

"You sure there's nothing else on your mind?" he asked as they headed onto a winding road that would ultimately lead to Cliff Lowe's home.

She shook her head. "No, really, I'm fine."

***

When John brought the car to a halt in Cliff Lowe's driveway, he immediately noticed a man hurrying down the steps to meet them.

"That's Cliff," Emma said, opening her car door.

"Good morning," Cliff said, sounding as if he'd already drunk half a pot of coffee.

"Good morning," John replied, holding out his hand. "I'm Agent John Milk."

They shook and then he reached for Emma. "Good morning, Agent Honeycutt."

"Good morning," she said. "The sheriff hasn't made it yet?"

"No. I admit I'm kind of surprised seeing you two here before him."

"Why is that?" John asked.

"Well, you work for the government and all," he said with a sly grin.

John and Emma looked at each other.

"I just mean the government is known to be slow and—"

"We get it, Mr. Lowe," Emma cut in. "You're quite witty this morning."

ROGUE

Cliff looked away sheepishly.

"How long of a hike are we looking at to get to this thing's den?" John asked.

"It'll take about half an hour on foot," he answered. "We could possibly go faster but we need to move slow to make sure it doesn't hear us coming."

It was then that Sheriff Cochran pulled up with two other deputy vehicles in tow. Once out of the vehicle, he moved to the trunk where he retrieved a shotgun and handed one to Billy, the deputy with the horn-rimmed glasses. The other deputies did the same, and soon Cliff was surrounded by armed local and federal law enforcement.

"Alright, I think we're all set," John said, doing his best to not sound anxious. The truth was, he *was* anxious and ready to see if Cliff could deliver on what he'd promised.

"Mr. Lowe, I think we need to be clear on something before we head out," Cochran said.

Cliff looked at him curiously. "Of course. What's on your mind, Sheriff?"

"All we're needing is for you to show us where this thing's den is. Once there, we need you to move aside and let us do our jobs. We'll tell you where to hang back and it's imperative that you stay where we tell you. I don't want you getting shot."

Cliff nodded but seemed a bit disappointed.

Emma, seemingly reading his thoughts, asked, "Mr. Lowe, you're not carrying a weapon, are you?"

His face told on him and he pulled up the tail of his red plaid shirt to reveal a pistol in his waistband.

"That's a nice Colt you've got there," Cochran said, holding out his hand.

Cliff sighed, but reluctantly handed the weapon over.

"You'll get it back when we finish this up," the sheriff said, shoving the gun into the back of his belt. He then looked past him to the woods behind the house. "We're ready when you are."

Cliff nodded and turned without saying a word. They all formed a single-file line and followed him into an opening that led into the forest. Emma and John made up the rear of the line.

***

As they traveled along the well-beaten path, John noticed the lack of sound. He knew it was early, but he expected to at least hear insects or birds chirping away. What he heard instead was nothing more than the soft footsteps in the pine straw and leaves that made up the forest floor.

"Is it just me or is it eerily quiet?" he whispered to Emma as she strode alongside him.

"No, it's not just you," she muttered quietly. "I've got a bad feeling about this, Milk."

He glanced at her. "Really? Why?"

She again considered mentioning her nightmare, but again kept quiet. "This just feels wrong," she replied. "I can't put my finger on why."

"Well, as you said earlier, we're in charge," he said. "If there's a reason we need to halt this, you need to speak up."

She shook her head. "No. I think I'm just a little edgy is all. I'll get over it."

He looked hard at her, trying to see if he could pick up anything from the expression on her face. She was a tough nut to crack at times and this was one of those times. He couldn't see a hint of anything on her face to give him an indication as to why she was "edgy."

"Just keep your eyes peeled and stay on your toes," he said. "We've got this."

She nodded and her eyes narrowed. "Damn, I need a cigarette."

John smiled. "The smoke would give us away."

"I know, I know," she grumbled.

Suddenly, the convoy of men ahead of them came to an abrupt stop.

"That's it," Cliff said quietly, pointing.

John and Emma moved briskly to where Cliff and the sheriff were standing.

"I don't see anything," John said.

"Me either," Cochran said.

Emma took another step forward. "Oh my God, I see it."

"There used to be a deep ditch that ran through here," Cliff explained. "That thing piled logs across the top of it and then covered it with straw and leaves. Perfect camouflage."

John squinted looked closely at the ground for any sign of a den that something could live in. After his eyes scanned the environment closely for almost a full minute, he finally spotted it.

"I see it," he muttered. "There's an opening there. It looks like it just goes into the ground. I assume that's the entrance?"

"That's right," Cliff said.

"How much room is inside there?" Cochran asked. He could apparently now see it too.

"I remember the ditch and it was deep," Cliff answered. "There's plenty of room in there."

"And you're sure it's in there?" Emma asked.

Cliff glanced at his watch. "Pretty sure, yes."

"So, what do you propose we do now, Agents?" Cochran asked, glancing at both John and Emma.

John clenched his jaw. He thought of Lucas' lifeless body he'd seen a short time ago. It angered him and he wanted to avenge the child's death. He wanted to make sure it never happened to another kid again.

"Let's go get it," he said, taking a step forward.

"Wait," Emma said, grabbing him by the bicep. "What do you mean 'let's go get it'?"

He pulled his sidearm and made sure a bullet was in the chamber. "I mean, we're going to go in there and kill it," he explained.

John could see something in Emma's eyes that he had not seen very often. It was fear. Seeing this troubled him and he decided he'd have to question her about it more later. For now, taking her into the wood ape's den in that state would not be wise.

"Emma, stay out here with Mr. Lowe," he said, trying to give her an out. "We'll go in there and if the thing's in there, it won't be alive much longer."

She looked at him, a mixture of anger and relief on her face. "You're sure you don't need me in there? I'm sure Mr. Lowe will—"

"I'm sure," he answered, cutting her off. "Stay with Mr. Lowe and we'll be back as soon as possible."

She sighed and for a moment, he thought she'd argue. Eventually, however, she pulled her own gun and said, "Alright, but hurry the hell up."

"Yes, ma'am," he replied, and John then led Cochran and his deputies to the entry of the wood ape's den.

As they drew near the entrance, a foul stench began to fill their nostrils.

"What the hell is that?" Billy asked, a little too loudly.

John halted when he heard the deputy speak and was terrified his carelessness had given them away. He kept his gun pointed into the entry before him as Cochran gave his deputy a vicious look that made it clear he was not to speak another word.

"Milk, do you think all of us should be going in there?" Sheriff Cochran asked.

John could hear the uncertainty in his tone.

"I think if there are more of us in there, then there are more guns in there," he replied. "More guns seem like the best option, don't you think?"

Cochran smiled and nodded. "Lead the way," he said, gesturing with his hand.

John inhaled deeply through his nose, but immediately regretted it when the foul odor made its presence known again.

Here goes nothing, he thought.

CHAPTER 6

As he entered the opening to the rogue wood ape's den, John realized it was extremely dark. He knew his eyes would adjust and help some, but he really needed extra light. Fortunately, Sheriff Cochran clicked a flashlight on behind him. John felt the ground underneath him slope downward as the darkness began to envelop him. He kept his gun pointed ahead of him and Cochran did the same with the beam originating from the flashlight. John's eyes stayed wide open; he was too afraid to even blink.

"God, the smell," Cochran whispered just behind him.

The smell *was* intense, and John, unfortunately, knew it well. It was the smell of death, and not just any death. Dead humans were what it was. As the other deputies closed in behind him, other flashlights flickered on and more of the wood ape's home became illuminated. It didn't take long to find out where the smell of death was originating. There were skulls everywhere and they were unmistakably human. Among the skulls were other bones of all kinds, all of them also human.

"Dear God," John said softly.

Sheriff Cochran and the other deputies shined their lights all around the enormous structure. All of it could be seen, and aside from articles of clothing, chunks of meat, and bloodstains, there was nothing else to be found.

"It's not here," Cochran said. "The damn thing isn't here."

John lowered his gun and slowly looked back at the sheriff. "Then where the hell is it?"

***

"Agent Honeycutt, are you able to see anything?" Cliff asked anxiously.

Emma had made him stay even further away, behind the trunk of a large oak tree.

"No, Mr. Lowe, I do not," she replied, somewhat aggravated.

She'd been angry with herself for allowing John to talk her into staying behind. He'd figured out she was afraid, and it infuriated her. She'd basically been relegated as babysitter for Cliff.

"Well, do you hear anything?" Cliff asked.

She rolled her eyes and sighed deeply. "No, Mr. Lowe, I do not."

"Do you think something is wrong?"

She was about to really lose her cool with him and turned around to let him have it, but a noise from somewhere to her right caught her attention.

"Did you hear that?" Cliff said, whipping his head around in the direction of the sound.

"Quiet," Emma whispered in a demanding tone.

She drew her gun and the two of them stood deadly still for what seemed like a full minute. Just as Emma was beginning to feel better about the situation, she caught a whiff of something that made her pulse quicken.

"Mr. Lowe, how does that thing smell?" she asked, trying to keep her composure.

Cliff didn't reply and when she turned to look at him, Emma immediately noticed his face was ashen. He was staring intensely at something behind her and to her right.

"Mr. Lowe," she said nervously. "Wh—what's wrong?"

Cliff was breathing hard, and his eyes were wide. Clearly, there was something behind her that was terrifying him.

"It's *him*," he muttered, slowing raising his hand, his finger pointing over her shoulder.

Emma swallowed hard and forced herself to turn and see what had terrified him so badly. When she did, the dark creature towering before her bolted for her with a quickness she had never expected. Emma had just enough time to fire her gun, but the wood ape seemed to expect it and spun out of the way just as she pulled the trigger. The beast then grabbed her arm and wrenched the weapon free from her grasp.

Emma fought the wood ape with all she had, and as the beast pulled her forward, she thrashed and kicked. It was all in vain. Before she even had time to register what was happening, the wood ape hooked an arm around her abdomen and bolted past Cliff into the nearby dense foliage. She could hear Cliff screaming for help, but his cries grew faint quickly, a testament to how quickly the beast moved away. A sinking feeling overcame her as she soon realized that by the time John and the others came out of the creature's den to investigate, she'd be long gone.

***

"What the hell happened?" John yelled as he ran quickly to where Cliff was standing. He noticed Emma's gun laying in the leaves at Cliff's feet and snatched it up.

"It took her!" he cried, clearly distraught.

Sheriff Cochran looked around in all directions, pointing his shotgun every which way he turned.

"Which way did they go?" he asked, a tone of fury overtaking his usual calm voice.

Cliff pointed to his right, his hand trembling. "It moved so fast."

Without hesitation, John bolted in the direction Cliff was pointing. He began yelling for Emma and to his dismay, he heard absolutely nothing in reply. The only sound he *did* hear was the footsteps of the sheriff and his deputies frantically trying to keep up with him.

"Milk!" Sheriff Cochran called after him. "I think we should split up, so we'll cover move ground!"

John didn't reply, but he could hear the men fan out in different directions behind him. He stayed straight and suddenly thought he'd heard a scream from somewhere far ahead.

"Honeycutt!" he yelled. "Are you out there?"

Every step he made crashed onto the leaves that covered the forest floor. It made hearing anything quite difficult. He strained his ears with all his might but despite his best efforts, he heard no reply to his calls. What he did hear, however, were more calls from Sheriff Cochran. He slowed his pace as he began to wonder if he or one of his deputies had found her. After mulling it over, he finally decided it best to stop and listen again. Panting, he leaned over, his hands on his knees. John expected to hear the sheriff again, but instead, he heard screaming.

***

Emma felt helpless but refused to give up her efforts to get free. The wood ape's hairy arm was large, and she could feel the bulge of its muscles pressing against her as it ran. She struck the creature with her fists until they hurt and grew numb. Even though the beast smelled horribly, her desperation drove her to bite its arm. To her utter dismay, the wood ape seemed to not even notice. Emma spat the foul taste from her mouth and continued to thrash wildly, hoping perhaps the beast would give up and drop her.

Suddenly, the wood ape *did* come to a stop and drop her to the ground. The fall was painful, but Emma hardly noticed. She used every precious second to claw at the earth to put as much distance between her and the creature as humanly possible. She struggled mightily to get to her feet and just as she was beginning to wonder if she'd injured one of her legs, she felt the wood ape's long fingers wrap around her ankle and yank her violently backward.

Emma began kicking her legs and it was at this moment she realized that one of them was indeed injured. She wasn't certain, but her right leg felt broken. A sharp pain began to radiate from her foot and all the way up to her hip. It seemed to grow more intense by the second.

"Get your damn hands off me!" she screamed, still furiously kicking at the beast's abdomen.

The wood ape soon had her dangling upside down as it stood straight and raised its arm high above its head. It's one good eye glared at her and she could clearly see the hatred behind it. The monster's mouth opened slightly, and Emma was able to see blood-stained teeth. She thought of Lucas Hurst and despite her best efforts to control it, her fear began to swell like a wildfire tearing through her core.

She knew what was coming. The wood ape's snarl and ugly expression spoke more than any words could. Its grip tightened around her ankle. Emma howled in pain and if she hadn't known better, she'd have believed someone was compressing a vise to torture her. The tightening continued as the creature squeezed tighter. Emma screamed louder, to the point she felt she was nearing unconsciousness. Then, suddenly, she was released and tumbled headfirst to the ground.

The blow to her head was severe and her neck bent awkwardly to one side. Emma was dazed to the point she was unable to move momentarily, but her eyes were open. Though momentarily blurred, her vision slowly came into focus to reveal that the beast had dropped her because it had been attacked. There was another wood ape squaring off with the one that had taken her. This one was slightly smaller, but it seemed undeterred by that fact.

Oh my God, it has green eyes…

The larger wood ape growled, and the sound Emma heard chilled her blood. It then sprang forward, leaping high and downward at her rescuer—the creature that had once been Kurt Bledsoe. The two beasts engaged in a heated, violent battle. The fight initially consisted of biting and numerous attempts at choking. Things then became more violent when the rogue wood ape grabbed a nearby rock and attempted to cave in Kurt Bledsoe's face. The attack was thwarted when Kurt reached up and grabbed the beast's arm as it swung down at him. Kurt then kicked the rogue wood ape between the legs, forcing the beast to roll off him. It howled in pain and rolled back and forth on the ground. Kurt then stood and tried to stomp on the beast as it writhed in agony. The rogue wood ape rolled out of the way just in time and somehow found the energy to regain its footing.

Kurt Bledsoe and the larger wood ape stood facing each other. Just as the two beasts prepared to engage in battle yet again, shots rang out from behind Kurt. Emma watched in horror as two bullets tore through the back of Kurt. The rogue wood ape took a back-handed swipe at its injured counterpart and sent Kurt hurtling to the ground beside Emma. It then tore through the forest, easily making an escape just as John made it to the scene.

He pointed his weapon at the head of Kurt Bledsoe but just as he was about to pull the trigger, Emma screamed for him to stop. Her words came off as a demand, not a plea. John was used to hearing this sort of tone from her, and though he was skeptical, it made him stop what he was doing.

"What the hell do you mean *stop*?" he yelled back at her, fury in his tone.

"This is Kurt Bledsoe!" she snapped back.

"No shit," he muttered in disbelief. "Weren't you just telling me that he's dangerous? I saw what was going on. He was going to kill you!"

"No! He was trying to *save* me from the rogue," she screamed at him as she attempted to get to her feet.

John could see her struggling and put a hand on a shoulder, forcing her to stay down. "Don't," he said. He then paused to peer over at Kurt. He was clearly injured and not a threat. John holstered his weapon and knelt beside Emma. He immediately noticed blood pooling around her right ankle.

"What happened to your leg?" he asked.

"Doesn't matter," she grumbled. "Stop holding me down and help me up."

John ignored her and pushed back her pants leg. As soon as he saw bone poking through the skin, he gasped.

"What?" she asked. "How bad is it?"

He glanced at her and knew it was no use in lying to her. "It's bad. Trust me and hold still."

Seconds later, Sheriff Cochran arrived. His eyes grew wide when he saw Kurt Bledsoe injured and bleeding on the ground in front of him.

"Did you shoot him?" he asked. He sounded disappointed.

"Yes," John said. "I thought he was hurting her."

"He wasn't?" Cochran asked.

"No, he wasn't!" Emma shouted, clearly frustrated that everyone assumed Kurt was trying to harm her. "He fought the rogue off."

"Sheriff, call some help for Honeycutt," John said. "She's injured."

"Of course," he answered. "But what about *him*?"

John looked over at Kurt Bledsoe.

"He saved my life," Emma said. "Get him patched up and hide him before Walker Laboratory shows up."

John glared at her, unable to believe what he was hearing.

"Are you serious right now?"

"You're damn right," she snapped back.

CHAPTER 7

Before becoming a dispatcher for the Baker County Sheriff's Department, Shelly Snow had worked as a receptionist and assistant to Dr. Fredrick Duvall at the veterinarian office in the Dunn town square. During her eleven years in that role, she picked up a lot of knowledge and experience on how to care for and treat wounded animals. Over the years, she'd occasionally treated pets that had been wounded by all sorts of means. There'd been dogs and cats that had suffered injuries from everything from car strikes to coyote attacks. With all the experience she'd acquired, nothing Shelly had ever done prepared her for the injured creature that was writhing in pain in the back of Sheriff Ray Cochran's patrol car. The wood ape barely fit in the car and it took up every square inch of space in the backseat.

The deputies pulled the cumbersome beast from the car and then carried it into the station. Cochran followed them and offered Shelly a smile as he strode past. It was a pathetic attempt to calm her and it failed to do the job by a long shot.

"Wh—what is that?" she stammered, following them all to the first holding cell inside the jail.

Cochran unlocked the door and swung it open, its tired hinges squeaking loudly in protest. Billy and the other deputies dropped the wood ape onto the concrete floor as carefully as possible. It was bleeding profusely from two gunshot wounds to its back.

Sheriff Cochran turned to her, placing both hands on her shoulders. "Shelly, you know exactly what this is," he said softly. "I need you to see if you can patch him up. Can you do that?"

Shelly was barely listening. Her attention was on the wood ape as it snapped and growled, clearly from the pain it was experiencing. Cochran shook her lightly.

"Shelly," he said, a little louder this time. "I need you to look at me."

She did as he asked, her eyes wide and foggy from the shock of it all.

"Can you patch him up?" he asked.

Shelly sighed. "I—I can try. I think so."

"Good," Cochran replied. He looked to Billy. "Get the first-aid kit and assist her with whatever she needs."

The deputy nodded and saw to the task. The sheriff turned his attention again to Shelly.

"No one is to know that this thing is back here," he told her sternly. "I've got to go check on something. I won't be gone long, but if anything happens, call the hospital. That's where I'll be."

Shelly looked at him curiously. "Is everything okay, Sheriff?" she asked. "Are those agents alright?"

He gave her a long stare that said more than any words he could've spoken. "I'll be back," he said, moving away from her.

Cochran headed for the exit and met Billy, first-aid kit in hand. "Remember what I said," he said, pointing at him. "No one is to know about Kurt Bledsoe."

"I got it, Sheriff," he said, briskly moving past him.

Cochran hurried to his patrol car and closed the rear door as it was still open from when they'd retrieved Kurt. He could see a great deal of blood on the backseat and there was a coppery smell in the air that made him nauseated. He then made his way to the opposite side of the car and as he reached for the driver's door handle, a white van came speeding into the parking lot. The van came to a screeching stop and the large side cargo door slid open. Three men spilled out of the interior, all dressed in solid white protective coveralls.

"Can I help you?" Cochran asked, making no effort to hide his annoyance.

"Yes, you can," a gray-haired, middle-aged man said. He was the tallest of the three men and he wore round spectacles. The frame of his glasses was blue, and it contrasted brightly against the white suit. The man was thin, and his hair formed a horseshoe around the sides of his head. "My name is Dr. Michael Emmerich and I'm here to collect the specimen."

Sheriff Cochran swallowed hard and stared at the man. He tried desperately to keep his cool. "Well, Dr. Emmerich, I don't know what creature you're here to collect, but whatever you're looking for isn't at my station."

Dr. Emmerich adjusted his glasses and his mouth was a straight line. "Sheriff, I know you're familiar with what we do over at Walker Laboratory. I was given the unfortunate task of replacing the late Dr. Franklin. I think you're also familiar with what happened to him?"

Cochran continued to stare at him, unblinking.

Dr. Emmerich sighed and continued when he realized Cochran wasn't going to respond. "Sheriff, I frankly don't have a lot of time. I need you to allow us passage into your station and assist us in getting the specimen into this van. We've been searching for it for quite a while."

Sheriff Cochran stepped toward Dr. Emmerich and placed his hands on his hips. The movement caused the bottom of his jacket to move back slightly, revealing his holstered pistol on his hip. Dr. Emmerich's eyes moved toward the weapon but he seemed undeterred.

"Doctor, I don't know where you get your information, but it's all wrong. Kurt Bledsoe isn't here. We've been on the hunt for a rogue wood ape that killed a young boy yesterday. As a matter of fact, we still are."

Dr. Emmerich pulled his glasses off and wiped the lenses on the chest of his coveralls before replacing them to his face. "Sheriff, I'm aware of the injury sustained by Agent Honeycutt. I'm also aware that Agent Milk fired two shots into the specimen, incapacitating him. The rogue wood ape is still out there. However, the specimen we've been after is not. Let's stop playing games here. Let me do my job."

Emmerich's words were nonchalant and had a coldness to them that Cochran didn't like.

"Okay, at this point, I think I'm going to have to ask you to leave," he said firmly.

Dr. Emmerich seemed surprised. "Sheriff, I don't think you understand your position here."

"Oh, I understand completely," Cochran shot back. "The federal government assigned two agents to act as liaison between my department and yours. They are not here, so I have no obligation to speak to you right now." He paused and moved his hand to the grip of his gun. "At this point, I'm going to have to ask you to leave."

Dr. Emmerich looked at him with an icy stare for a long awkward moment. After considering his position, he glanced at his two accomplices and gestured for them to return to the van. "I'll be back soon," he said through clenched teeth. "If the creature dies, I will hold you personally responsible."

"You have a good night," Cochran replied, tipping his hat.

He watched as the doctor slunk away into the van and shortly after, it sped away as quickly as it had appeared. Once satisfied they were truly gone, Cochran got into his car and took off for the hospital.

***

"You refused to grant them access?" John asked, his reaction a mixture of surprise and worry.

"That's exactly what I did," Cochran replied. "They showed up out of the blue. And I thought the whole idea was that we were gonna get Kurt out of there before Walker Laboratory showed up for him."

"Well, yeah," John replied. "But if they found out about that you have him, there's not a lot we can do at that point. You should've allowed them entry."

"I told them I wasn't doing anything unless you and Honeycutt gave the okay."

John considered that and nodded. "Actually, I think that was probably the best way to handle it. It probably aggravated the hell out of him, but he understands the deal. Honeycutt and I work for the federal government just as they do. Ultimately, it wasn't his call if we weren't involved."

Sheriff Cochran exhaled with relief. He was glad to hear that John was okay with what he'd done, as he was beginning to wonder if there was anything he could do to please these people.

"How is Honeycutt?"

John leaned against the wall and crossed his arms. They were in a small hospital waiting room. There was no one else in the room and the only other sound was Richard Dawson holding court on *Family Feud* displayed on a television blaring in a faraway corner.

"She's alright," he muttered. "You know her...she's ready to get out of here and get back to work. It's going to require surgery to fix her leg so she's going to be in here for a few days."

Cochran nodded. "Well, we've got Kurt Bledsoe in a jail cell at the station. Shelly is working on him. She's got some experience with this sort of thing, so I'm confident she'll have him patched up in no time."

John glanced out the windows around the room to the hallway outside. He was very careful to make sure no one was outside listening. Once satisfied, he moved closer to Cochran.

"We'll have to turn him over to Walker Laboratory tomorrow," he said.

The sheriff thought about it, then said, "I don't think we need to move him anywhere until we're sure he's healthy enough."

John glared at him, obviously confused. "What are you talking about, Sheriff? Why do you care what happens to him?"

Cochran's eyes narrowed. "I care because if it wasn't for him, I'd have died last year in that damn laboratory. I promised his sister that I'd do what I could to look out for him."

John paced the room with his hands on his hips. "I think you're still under the assumption that things are going to be done the way Dr. Franklin was doing them. That's just not accurate. You have my word that the best place for Kurt Bledsoe is in that lab."

"Would Agent Honeycutt agree?"

John sighed. "Up until this morning, hell yes she would've."

"But now?"

He shook his head. "No. She feels she owes him something now because he saved her life from the rogue."

"So, I think we should discuss this with her," Cochran said hopefully.

"It is not her call, Sheriff."

Sheriff Cochran held his hands up. "Okay, okay," he said. "Look, you guys are running the show here. Halloween is in two days, and me and my guys will have our hands full. I propose you reach out to Walker Laboratory and set up a time for us to transport him over on November first. That'll give Kurt Bledsoe time to heal up and we'll actually have the time to deal with it."

John considered it for a moment before finally nodding. "I'll see what I can do. Speaking of Halloween, have you considered the dangers involved with that rogue wood ape on the loose out there with hundreds of kids out trick or treating?"

Cochran rubbed at the back of his neck and took a deep breath. "Yeah, I've thought about it," he said, clearly concerned. "We need to come up with another plan."

"We need to go speak with Cliff Lowe again," John said. "I'm sure he's got some ideas on where we should go from here."

"Good idea," Cochran said. "I think I'll go pay him a visit."

John nodded. "You do that, and I'll call Dr. Emmerich to see what I can work out with him."

***

Cliff Lowe was sitting on his front porch when Sheriff Cochran pulled into the driveway. He smiled when he saw the large boxy patrol car and Cochran wondered if he'd known all along he'd be coming by.

"How is Agent Honeycutt?" he asked as he walked out to meet the sheriff at the car.

"She's going to be fine," Cochran said. "Her leg is going to require some surgery, but she'll be alright."

Cliff's eyes widened and Cochran could see he was relieved to hear the news.

"Look, we appreciate all the help you gave us today," he said. "But as you know, that damn thing is still on the loose."

Cliff nodded and smiled widely. "I'm already ahead of you, Sheriff."

Cochran hooked his thumbs in his pants pockets and rocked on his heels. "So, you've been thinking about this?"

"Yes, I have. I've got an idea," he said proudly.

CHAPTER 8

"This is it? This is your idea?" Cochran asked skeptically.

Cliff nodded but seemed slightly hurt by the sheriff's reaction. "I've been thinking of doing this for quite some time," he said. "I just figured I needed some help before I actually attempted it. Unfortunately, I don't have too many friends around here. Everyone kinda thinks I'm nuts."

He was holding a massive bear trap in his right hand. At his feet were four more of the rusty contraptions. They were old and dirty, and Cochran wondered if they'd even work.

"Well, I certainly don't think you're nuts," the sheriff replied assuredly. "And though I'm thankful for your enthusiasm, are you sure those traps are still functional?"

Cliff smiled as if he were glad that Cochran wanted to test him. The sheriff looked on as the much smaller man straddled the trap, placing one foot on either side of it to compress the springs. He then knelt and used a long shaft screwdriver to set the trigger from underneath the wide-open jaws. The process looked extremely dangerous to Cochran, but it seemed Cliff had practiced this method many times before. Satisfied that the trap was set correctly, Cliff then retrieved a sizeable tree branch lying on the ground a short distance away.

"Okay, are you watching?" he asked, sounding like a kid that had just learned a new trick he wanted to show off.

Cochran smiled. "I'm ready."

Cliff promptly dropped the branch onto the plate in the center of the trap. The jaws immediately snapped shut with so much force it tore through the wood like it was cardboard.

"Satisfied?" he asked, grinning.

The sheriff allowed a tight smirk and nodded. "Alright, so where do we place them?"

Cliff walked back over to his front porch and retrieved two duffel bags. He tossed Cochran one. "Put two of the traps in that bag," he said.

Cochran did as he was told, zipped up the bag, and placed the strap over his shoulder. He was immediately surprised at how heavy it was.

"How much do these things weigh?"

"Around forty pounds each," Cliff replied, now carrying his own bag. "Follow me."

Sheriff Cochran considered asking more questions but realized Cliff clearly knew more about how to deal with the wood ape than he did. Ultimately, he decided to practice trust and follow the man into the woods. The walk was long and grueling, more so than the first time Cochran had ventured to the wood ape's den. It was probably because of the eighty pounds he was lugging around on his shoulder. As they drew near the wood ape's home, Cochran began to feel a bit uneasy. He was just about to voice his concern when Cliff stopped and dropped his bag to the ground. The sheriff did the same and then massaged the burning sensation out of his tired shoulder.

"I doubt it's in there right now," Cliff said, seemingly reading Cochran's thoughts. "We spooked it earlier today."

"Well, how do you know it'll come back?"

"Oh, it'll come back," Cliff said confidently. "It's seen me watching it here before."

Sheriff Cochran was a bit taken aback. "You're sure it's seen you watching it?"

Cliff nodded. "Yes, and you can bet that it wants to kill me very badly."

"Then why doesn't it?"

"It knows I took its eye," he answered. "I think it's got a healthy respect for me."

Cochran swatted at an insect swarming around his head. Somehow, he thought Cliff's assumption was incorrect, but he wasn't about to argue the matter.

"Anyway," Cliff continued. "It'll come back because it thinks it's invincible."

"I see," Cochran answered. That part he did believe. "So why do you think it's turned rogue?"

Cliff shrugged. "I've often wondered about that. I think maybe it was banished because it's made a habit of getting close to humans for a while now. I think it's been working its way up to taking a human and once it got a taste of flesh…"

"To my knowledge, Lucas Hurst is the first case—"

"You're telling me you haven't had any missing person cases in the past few years?" Cliff interrupted.

Sheriff Cochran considered the question. A chill ran up his spine. "We've had a few," he admitted. "Too many."

Cliff nodded but said nothing. He instead knelt and opened the bag he'd carried. He pulled the heavy bear traps out along with some clothing.

"What's that for?" Cochran asked.

"This is bait," Cliff replied, holding up an old Spuds Mackenzie T-shirt.

Cochran looked at the shirt and then to Cliff. "I don't get it."

Cliff grinned and carried a trap toward the entrance of the wood ape den. "These are intelligent creatures," he said, dropping the trap to the ground. He then went about setting it. "It's not a rat after a piece of cheese. These things are very fascinated by humans and are notorious for picking up all sorts of items we discard. I think our rogue wood ape would be interested in checking out a T-shirt with Spuds on it."

"Sure. Who wouldn't want a Spuds Mackenzie T-shirt?" Cochran asked.

He looked on as Cliff carefully situated the shirt in such a way that the trap was completely hidden but in a perfect position to make it easy to go off. He then drove a spike into the base of a nearby tree trunk to secure the anchor. That part he covered with pine straw. Cochran had to admit that it was a job well done.

"So same plan for the other traps?" he asked.

Cliff nodded and began rummaging through the bag. Cochran could see other T-shirts inside. "I've got Thundercats, A.L.F., Michael Jackson—"

"I got it," Cochran said with a chuckle. "Just let me know how I can help."

Cliff nodded but stubbornly refused to ask for any help as he continued to strategically place and set the traps.

***

"Agent Milk, you're fortunate I don't make a call to your superior right this instant," the doctor said bitterly.

John winced as he'd expected such a threat. "Dr. Emmerich, there's no need to call Mr. Cold. The last contact I had with him, he'd mentioned something about an island he was investigating in the heart of the Bermuda Triangle."

There was a pause on the other end of the line. "In the middle of the Bermuda Triangle, you say?"

"That's right," John confirmed. "He called it a 'Lost World' that he was trying to locate. I didn't ask him any questions. You know how he is."

"Yes, I suppose I do," Emmerich said. "So, if what you say is true, I suppose I'd have a hard time reaching him anyway." He sounded aggravated but John pretended not to notice.

"It would take a couple of days," he said, gripping the phone tightly. "Look, Dr. Emmerich, I'm not trying to step on any toes here. However, you and I both know that if we can keep the peace with local law enforcement, we need to do that."

"I can't risk losing that specimen," Emmerich said coldly.

"You won't," John replied quickly. "No one is trying to pull any tricks here. I spoke with Sheriff Cochran a short time ago and he simply requested that we leave Kurt Bledsoe in his custody until November first."

"That day after Halloween?"

"Yes," John replied, not really understanding the point of the question.

"It still doesn't make any sense to me. We could provide much better care for it. If the specimen is injured, I don't want to risk anything happening to it that we could've prevented."

"Is there a reason why you refer to Kurt Bledsoe as 'the specimen'?"

There was another brief pause on the other end of the line. "It's not Kurt Bledsoe anymore," Emmerich replied. "Maybe it's you that should change your perception of what the creature is."

John let out an exasperated sigh. "I understand your concerns and I'll take on the responsibility to seeing to it that…the specimen, is delivered to you in good health. If I don't think that can happen, you'll be the first to know and I'll make arrangements for you and your men to come get it."

"And why can't you do that now?" Emmerich asked, evidently refusing to let the matter rest.

"Tomorrow is Saturday," John answered. "And it's not just any Saturday, it's Halloween. There are going to be people all over Dunn and the laboratory you work for goes to great lengths to stay out of the public eye as much as possible. As a matter of fact, I've been told on more than one occasion that if you guys had your way, no one in this county would know that it existed."

"That's a true statement," the doctor confirmed. There was another pause and it was his turn to sigh. "Agent Milk, do you understand the consequences for you and me both if something happens to that creature?"

"I do," John said, doing his best to hide the uneasy feeling swelling inside him. "You have my word that the specimen will be delivered to you first thing Sunday morning. I won't let any harm come to it."

"Very well," Emmerich said reluctantly. "I suppose I have no reason to doubt you at this point."

"No, you don't," John said. He opened his mouth to speak again but then thought better of it. There was a long awkward silence.

"Something else on your mind, Agent Milk?" Emmerich asked curiously.

John waited a beat longer before finally deciding it wouldn't hurt to broach the subject. "What about the rogue wood ape?" he asked.

"What about it?"

"Are you not concerned about it? I mean, why are you people not putting forth just as much effort to catch it as you are Kurt Bledsoe?"

"I suggest you ask Sheriff Cochran that same question," Emmerich answered. "He knows better than most that studying wood apes is nothing new to us. However, studying a human/wood ape hybrid is a much different ball game."

"So, you're not going to help us?" John asked, almost pleadingly. "The thing killed a kid."

"And that is concerning," Dr. Emmerich said. "Actually, if I were you…"

His words trailed off as if he'd reconsidered what he was going to say.

"What?" John asked, urging him to continue. "If you were me…what?"

"Well," Emmerich said, and he paused again as if he were considering the best way to phrase the statement.

"Spit it out," John said impatiently.

"Very well. I was just going to say, given the fact that this particular wood ape is rogue and has seemingly now developed a taste for human flesh—a child's flesh specifically…I just think perhaps Halloween would not be a good idea this year."

John considered what he'd said a moment, trying to understand. "Are you saying we should cancel Halloween in Dunn this year?"

"There will be a lot of young children out and about collecting candy," Dr. Emmerich said matter-of-factly.

"So, you think this thing is going to go after another child as soon as it gets the chance?"

"I'm saying it's a good possibility," Emmerich replied. "It wouldn't be a popular decision to cancel the evening festivities, but is it worth the gamble?"

John felt a headache coming on. He hadn't considered any of what the doctor was saying but he had to admit that it made a lot of sense.

"Thanks for your insight," John said. "I'll have your specimen ready to go first thing November first."

"We will be there at eight a.m."

"Understood," John answered.

All he got was dial tone in response.

CHAPTER 9

"I can't let you do that," Sheriff Cochran said, his face stern and expressionless.

Cliff's jaw dropped open and he held his hands out, palms up. "Sheriff, how is anyone supposed to know if we trap the thing if I don't hang around?"

Cochran shook his head. "How are we supposed to know the thing has been trapped when you're dead and can't tell us?"

"Sheriff, this would not be my first time to hide and watch," Cliff continued. His eyes were wide and pleading. His tone wasn't frustration but more helpless.

Cochran sighed as he contemplated what Cliff was suggesting. As much as he didn't want to admit it, it would be extremely helpful to have someone nearby to monitor the traps. If the wood ape was caught, they'd have to move very quickly.

"Alright," the sheriff said finally, his voice full of reluctance. "I suppose you know far more about this thing than I ever will."

Cliff smiled and nodded in agreement. "When we catch it, you'll be the first to know."

Cochran bit his lip. "I better be," he muttered, turning away.

***

Emma shifted in her bed uncomfortably, her face contorting from the pain. "No, absolutely not," she grumbled while the bed squeaked. "There is no way in hell we're going to cancel Halloween."

John drew near her and placed a hand on her shoulder. "Please sit still," he said. "The more you rest, the quicker you'll get back on your feet."

She seemed to ignore him. "Although, I have to admit that bastard Emmerich makes some good points. We should start making plans with the sheriff to make a strict curfew on Halloween."

John nodded and refrained the urge to roll his eyes at her ignoring him.

"And I think it's a good idea to contain trick or treating to the town square. It'll give us a tighter area to control."

"I don't know if that'll go over well with the people of this county," John said.

She sighed and rubbed her eyes. "Yeah, you're probably right," she said. "And I can't say that I blame them."

"Well, up until now, the presence of wood apes in the area has been more or less a myth," John said. "The disappearance and death of Lucas Hurst has changed all that. People are talking and they know what's going on. I believe if we start declaring martial law here, it's going to do nothing but ratchet up their fears even more."

"So, you're saying we do nothing?"

He considered it a moment, then said, "I think your idea about a curfew is a good idea. Outside of that, I think that the sheriff's department needs to patrol every area with a heavy presence of trick or treaters. We should try to give the illusion that things are as normal as we can. Mr. Cold wouldn't want us bringing unnecessary attention to any of the paranormal goings on here. He'd want us to try and eliminate that attention."

"You're right," Emma agreed. She then looked down at her leg, wrapped in a heavy cast.

"So, you're going to be wearing that for several weeks?"

"Yes," she grumbled. "I suppose I shouldn't complain. I should be happy to be alive."

"Yeah, you should," John replied.

"How is Kurt Bledsoe?" she asked.

"He's resting comfortably in a jail cell," he answered. "Shelly has some experience working in a vet. Turned out to be a big help."

"Well, isn't that convenient?"

"I'd say so," John said. "He'll be safe there for now, but as of November first, we will have to turn him over to Walker Laboratory."

Emma turned away and her face turned a bit somber. "I owe him my life," she said. "Do you think they will take care of him?"

"I do," he answered. "They wanted to take him immediately, but I didn't think it was a good idea. Once he's healed and in that lab, you and I are going to check up on him regularly to make sure they do what they say they're going to do."

"And if they don't?"

"Then we get Cold involved," John said. "He'll make sure that they do."

Emma nodded, seemingly happy with that response. "Halloween is tomorrow. There isn't a lot of time to prepare," she said.

"We're back to that again, are we?" John asked, placing his hands in his coat pockets.

"Sorry, I just can't get it out of my head," she replied. "I've got a bad feeling about it."

John shifted his feet and then decided to sit on the edge of the bed near her injured leg. "Look, Sheriff Cochran *already* had big plans for him and his men to be on patrol throughout the night. All we need to do now is get a little more organized on the specifics of this effort and what the contingency plan is if things go bad."

"Do you think things will go bad?"

"No," he replied without hesitation. "I don't. As a matter of fact, Cochran has been consulting with Cliff Lowe on the matter. No one knows that thing better than he. Perhaps he'll know something that we can use to our benefit to make it a non-issue."

She screwed up her face. "You've got to be kidding me."

"What?" he asked, confused.

"We're not placing the fate of hundreds of children in the hands of Clifford Lowe," Emma said.

"Of course not," John scoffed. "But it's a start."

He glanced down at the white cast wrapped around Emma's leg then retrieved a black marker from his coat pocket.

"I came prepared," he muttered as he pulled the cap off with his teeth.

Emma smiled and looked on as he signed his name in big block letters.

***

"How is he?" Sheriff Cochran asked the second he walked through the front door of the station.

"Resting," Shelly said, rising to meet him. "Sheriff, I've never seen anything like that. Are we in danger here keeping that thing in the building?"

Cochran smiled at her and gave her a pat on the back. "It's fine, trust me," he assured her.

He began to walk away, but then paused to look back at her. "Are you alright?" he asked.

She looked back at him and he could see the tiredness in her eyes. "I'm fine, Sheriff," she said. "It's just a lot to take in."

He sighed, removed his hat, and then turned it in his hands as he considered what to say next. He knew he could trust Shelly, but what she'd just been through and saw was more than he'd ever wanted her to endure.

"Shelly, I apologize, but I have to ask…"

"Sheriff, I'm not going to say a thing," she answered, knowing full well what he was going to ask. "You know better than to assume anything different."

He nodded and forced another smile. "Go home and get some rest," he said. "I'm going to need you here tomorrow. It's going to be a busy day."

Shelly stared a moment and he feared briefly she was going to argue. "Alright," she said finally. "I'll be back first thing tomorrow. If something changes with the…"

"I'll call you if I need you," Cochran said. "I'm sure everything will be fine until morning."

She nodded, then retrieved her purse and left the building.

After making a brief stop in his office to review the mail that had been left on his desk, Cochran headed for the jail cell where Kurt Bledsoe would be resting and healing from his wounds. The cell was usually reserved for use as a drunk tank, and it was the first one to see upon visiting the jail. Cochran placed his hands on the bars and leaned forward. The wood ape that Kurt Bledsoe had become didn't have the same smell as the other ones he'd encountered. Though it wasn't a pleasant smell, it was nowhere near intolerable or sickening. The dark fur on Kurt's chest rose and fell with each breath his new frame took.

Cochran thought back to the events of nearly a year ago. He remembered the horrifying situation he found himself in once he'd become trapped deep in the bowels of Walker Laboratory. It was there where Kurt Bledsoe saved his life by taking on an alien creature that he still had trouble believing was real.

Kurt suddenly moved, rolling slightly onto his side. He was laying on the floor with a rolled-up towel serving as a makeshift pillow under his head. He made a slight growl when he moved, and Cochran could tell it originated from pain. He was just about to walk away when Kurt rolled again, this time toward him. His green eyes flickered open and there was a long moment where the two of them stared at one another.

"I suppose I've never taken a moment to properly thank you," Cochran said. He slowly knelt so he'd be closer to where Kurt was laying. The green eyes followed him. "I want you to know that Marie is fine. She moved over to New Orleans. She just had to get away. She said you'd understand."

Kurt blinked but his mouth remained a straight line. Though there was no response that Cochran could see, it was very apparent that Kurt was listening to his every word.

"And you're probably wondering about your best friend Tony," he continued. "He's good. He's attending college at State. Every time I speak to him, he asks if I've seen any sign of you. I can't wait until the next time he asks me that question."

Kurt continued to stare.

"Damn, I wish you could talk," Cochran said, a tad frustrated. "I wish you could tell me what you know of the rogue. I'm sure you know something that would help us out."

Kurt's eyes widened and his brow furrowed slightly at the mention of the rogue wood ape.

"Sore subject, I see," Cochran said with a chuckle. "I appreciate you taking him on to protect Agent Honeycutt. She wouldn't be here anymore if it weren't for you."

His expression softened as he continued to listen to the sheriff.

"Kurt, I'm fairly certain that you understand me, so hear this," he said, moving his face a bit closer to the bars. "In a couple of days, I'm going to be forced to hand you back over to Walker Laboratory. How do you feel about that?"

Kurt moved his massive head upward so he could look at the ceiling of the cell. All at once, his entire demeanor seemed to change at the mention of the laboratory.

"You're not keen on that idea," Cochran said as he watched.

For a long moment, he didn't know what to say. He just watched Kurt lay there, staring at the ceiling.

"I'm sorry, Kurt. I'm so sorry that this has happened to you."

Kurt closed his eyes tightly and the sheriff looked on sadly as a single tear rolled down the young man's new face.

CHAPTER 10

Cliff Lowe found a comfortable log to sit on and stayed there for the remainder of the day. It became quite a chore to keep his eyes open, but he was determined to stay focused on watching and listening for the rogue wood ape that was responsible for murdering Lucas Hurst. While he waited, Cliff did something he didn't ordinarily do. He took in the sights before him and made a point to observe his beautiful surroundings. He took a deep breath and his nose picked up the scent of pine. It was truly a wonderful place for one to sit and think, he decided. Over the years, he'd spent so much time watching the wood ape and studying its habits that he had completely forgotten the beauty and solitude that the forest provided. It was good for the soul.

Despite his newfound appreciation for the forests of Baker County, Mississippi, Cliff found himself often yawning. His eyelids began to grow more and more heavy. There were many times he considered taking a brief nap, but he knew full well the danger such a careless act would bring. Cliff also knew that Sheriff Cochran was depending on him to alert him to any sightings of the rogue wood ape as soon as possible. He had traps set, sure, but he was not completely sure just how effective they would be.

As the minutes and hours ticked by, the sun drifted further into the western sky. Before long, the world around him began to darken. To his dismay, the wood ape seemingly stayed away from its den for the remainder of the day. Cliff began to accept that the creature probably would not be returning until the morning. After some careful consideration, he decided that he would be unable to see the wood ape return at sunrise if he is asleep. With reluctance, he finally trudged back to his home, ultimately deciding a few hours of sleep in his bed would do him good.

Cliff took a quick shower, brushed his teeth, and then put on the clothes he planned on wearing the following day. When he awoke from his slumber, there would be no time to waste. He'd simply roll out of bed and head straight into the forest to check the traps. Minutes after his head hit the pillow, he was snoring and fast asleep.

***

The annoying repetitive tone of the alarm clock on the nightstand next to him caused Cliff to sit up immediately upon hearing it. Just as he'd planned, Cliff grabbed a heavy coat and then headed into the cool, damp air just moments before twilight. He shoved his right hand into his coat pocket and felt the cool steel of the Colt 45 in his palm. His hand on the weapon seemed to give him comfort and strangely kept the building anxiety he'd been experiencing in check. As he neared the area where the wood ape den would be found, he noticed how eerily quiet the forest had become. It was normal for that time of the morning, he knew, but there was a tension in the air that seemed to suggest something else was contributing to the lack of sounds.

When the entry of the den came into view, Cliff glanced over at the first trap he'd set only to find it had not been tripped. The other traps were difficult to see in the dim light and he soon realized he'd have to get closer. He had not been so nervous about venturing near the den when Sheriff Cochran had been with him. Another set of eyes— and a man with a gun—had made him a lot more comfortable.

Cliff pulled the Colt 45 from his pocket for the first time. With careful steps, he padded across the leaves and pine straw to make as little noise as possible so he could get a visual on the other traps. The next one that came into view was still set just as the first one had been. Cliff sighed and began to wonder if the entire effort had been in vain. He felt his heart rate increase as he moved past the entry of the creature's den, but it was necessary to get a good look at the next trap. It too was still set, but something else caught his eye that gave him a chill. The leaves on the ground were splattered with something dark and wet. It was clearly blood.

The sight made Cliff stop dead in his tracks as he began to realize that one of the traps had indeed worked. The location of the blood, however, gave him another unsettling realization. The trap may have indeed been tripped by the wood ape, but it was apparently unsuccessful in keeping the beast immobilized. Slowly, Cliff began to back away. Suddenly, he couldn't help but wonder what he was doing there in the first place. It had only been four years ago when the very beast he was trying to trap had grabbed him and nearly killed him.

What the hell am I doing?

Cliff turned and his brisk walk evolved into a jog. The desire to keep his movements quiet had disappeared and were now replaced with his instinctual desire to stay alive. As he again made his way past the entry to the wood ape's den, a low growl erupted from within the primitive structure. The sound was sinister and terrifying. Cliff began to run, and no sooner had he begun to hit his stride, the wood ape burst from within the den. It threw both of its long arms above its head and released a terrifying howl of rage.

Cliff could not resist the urge to look over his shoulder as he ran. The wood ape glared at him and it was obvious the creature remembered that Cliff was the person responsible for the loss of one of its eyes. The jaws of one of the bear traps was clamped down onto the right wrist of the wood ape. Its hairy arm was matted with blood and the large hand was enveloped to the point that it was useless. Despite the beast's injury, Cliff knew firsthand that it was quick and there would be almost no chance of outrunning it if it decided to go after him.

Cliff tried to put the thought out of his head and concentrated on the narrow trail ahead of him. He could hear the wood ape chasing after him, its large feet crashing violently against the forest floor with every step. Cliff dared not look back and tried with all his might to run at a faster pace. The wood ape quickly closed the gap and Cliff could sense the creature preparing to grab him from behind. He quickly turned his body and pointed the Colt 45 the lumbering beast bearing down on him. Cliff pulled the trigger and the thunderous blast expelled a bullet that struck the wood ape in the chest. To his surprise and relief, the wood ape's pace slowed down and Cliff managed to pull away again, leaving the injured beast behind in the forest.

***

Sheriff Cochran brought the large patrol car to an abrupt halt upon entering Cliff Lowe's driveway. He emerged from the vehicle and the trailing dust cloud overtook him as he quickly strode toward the house.

"Is it still out there?" he asked, unable to contain his excitement.

Cliff nodded. "I think so," he said.

He was seated in a rocking chair on the front porch of his home. The Colt was lying across his lap and his face was ashen.

"Are you alright?"

Cliff nodded, his eyes wide. "It came after me," he muttered.

Cochran approached him and patted him on the shoulder. "You did well," he said. "And most importantly, you didn't get killed."

Cliff chuckled uneasily and rose to his feet. "I suppose we should head back."

"No," Cochran said. "You've been a big help. I think I'll take it from here."

Cliff nodded but seemed clearly disappointed. "I don't feel like I've done anything."

The sheriff clutched his shoulder and moved so he could look Cliff in the eyes. "Mr. Lowe, do you know what today is?"

Cliff nodded. "Halloween," he said in a voice just above a whisper.

"That's right. Tonight, the town of Dunn will be overtaken by children out trick or treating."

"Yeah," Cliff replied, somewhat confused.

Cochran smiled and went on to explain. "If you've incapacitated that thing, there are going to be a lot of kids tonight that will be far safer than they would've been if it was still on the loose."

"Well, it hasn't been caught yet," he responded with a worried expression.

The sheriff sighed and gently forced Cliff back into his rickety rocking chair. "That's true," he said. "So, I better get going. You sit tight and I'll be back in a minute."

Cliff nodded and resumed rocking. "Be careful, Sheriff."

Cochran said nothing but turned away and retreated into the woods. It was now mid-morning and though the sun had warmed the air enough to where he could no longer see his own breath, the sheriff kept his heavy coat on to stay comfortable. As he walked, he couldn't help but notice the eerie silence around him. Though he was unable to put his finger on what exactly was causing it, Cochran could feel anxiety trying to overtake him. He'd seen and endured a lot over the past year where wood apes and other paranormal creatures were concerned but despite that fact, it was nearly impossible for him to shake the feeling of an impending doom looming just ahead of him.

For a moment, he considered turning back. Perhaps he'd be better off calling for one of his deputies to assist. However, he also knew this would take time. More time would increase the odds that the wood ape would somehow find a way to escape despite its injuries. This was a critical moment in providing safety to Baker County on one of its most vulnerable nights of the year. Cochran pushed the wavering thoughts from his mind and pressed onward. He wondered how much searching he'd have to do to find the dangerous creature. In his mind, he anticipated the search taking a bit of time. He assumed there would be a blood trail to follow. Cochran's mind then wandered to what he was going to do when he found the beast.

With a little luck, the damn thing will be dead.

No sooner did the wood ape's den come into view did the current questions in Cochran's mind find their answers. Before him, and sprawled across the forest floor mere feet from the entry to the den, lay the rogue wood ape. Cochran was slightly taken aback at the site of the creature. He'd expected it to take a bit longer than what it did to locate it. The thing was not moving though he could clearly see it was alive as its chest rose and fell with each rattled breath it took. It had lost a lot of blood but somehow, the creature still lived.

Sheriff Cochran eyed it for a moment as he contemplated what to do next. The thing's stench filled the air and he had to stifle the urge to wretch as he moved near it. Cochran pointed the barrel of his gun directly at the wood ape's head as he used his other hand to retrieve handcuffs from his belt.

"I hope these things fit you," he muttered, reaching for the wood apes' left wrist.

To his utter amazement, the cuff fit the wrist, but just barely. The creature's hair was coarse and matted with mud and dirt, but it was nothing compared to the mess that comprised the right wrist. Cochran studied the gnarly looking bear trap that was snapped tight on the beast's right wrist. There would be no placing the other cuff around it with the trap in the way. The hair was matted heavily with dried blood and it seemed to still be oozing more. Much to his dismay, he didn't see any way to remove the trap unless he used both of his hands to do so. Even then, it was going to be a chore.

With great reluctance, Cochran returned his gun to the holster on his belt. He then straddled the wood ape's arm and began the tedious task of pulling it free. After a great deal of struggling, the sheriff somehow managed to get his fingers under the jaws of the trap. His hands were suddenly covered in warm blood and it made it somewhat difficult to get a good grip. After a few attempts, he finally managed to grab the jaws of the trap and pull hard enough to open it just enough to slide it off the wood ape's arm. With the beast free, Cochran dropped the trap and the exhaustion that derived from the ordeal caused him to inadvertently tumble to the ground.

"Damnit," he spat as he quickly regained his footing.

With a quickness that belied his age, Cochran turned his attention back to the wood ape and he again drew his sidearm. The beast remained unconscious and the sheriff laughed as he considered how terrified he must've looked. After regaining his composure, he set to work on cuffing the gory mess that remained of the wood ape's right wrist. He once again straddled the massive creature's arm and hooked the cool steel under the hairy wrist. Unfortunately, the normally quick motion of locking the cuff wasn't quick enough. The wood ape suddenly jarred awake, yanking its arm away from the sheriff.

Cochran was startled by the lightning speed and he clumsily fell forward to the ground again. The gun he'd been holding broke free of his grip and tumbled a few feet away in the leaves ahead of him. The sheriff wasted no time to see what the wood ape was doing and instead put all his attention on retrieving the gun. He crawled quickly over to it, reaching it in mere seconds. Just as his fingertip touched the grip, Cochran felt a vice-like pressure clamp down on his ankle and yank him backward.

Before he'd even had a chance to register what was happening, Cochran found himself hanging upside down and looking directly into the face of pure evil. The wood ape was standing, holding onto his ankle with its good hand. Cochran's hat fell from his head and he frantically began trying to shove a hand in his pocket to retrieve his pocketknife. The wood ape, seemingly aware of what he was doing, opened its fanged mouth and released a terrifying roar that chilled the sheriff's blood.

CHAPTER 11

The wood ape's breath was hot, and the odor was putrid. Sheriff Cochran was fully aware he was moments away from his death. Surprisingly, he wasn't as frightened as he thought he would be. He'd seen firsthand what these beasts were capable of and he knew if there was any chance of survival, there was no time to ponder it. Cochran's fingers finally found the pocketknife he'd been searching for, and he quickly pulled it from his pants pocket and opened it up. With no hesitation, Cochran plunged it forward into the creature's chest. The wood ape roared in response and though Cochran's effort had apparently inflicted pain, the beast's reaction seemed to come more from rage than pain.

The wood ape continued to hold him upside down with a painful grip that caused his foot to go completely numb. The now angry beast used its free hand to pull the blade free from its flesh. It studied the knife with its good eye and snarled furiously as it tossed it to the ground. Cochran used the moment of distraction to use his fists to pummel the wood ape in the center of its chest, but the effort was to no avail. The beast drew back and threw the sheriff into the air like a frisbee. Cochran struck the trunk of an oak tree with his shoulder and he fell painfully to the earth. He yowled in pain, immediately sensing that the shoulder had become dislocated from its socket.

The wood ape showed no empathy and strode toward him with purpose. Cochran could see a steady trickle of blood emitting from the knife wound he'd given the beast, but to his dismay, the wood ape didn't even seem to notice. Cochran attempted to get to his feet, but he simply was not quick enough. Once the wood ape reached him, it reached down and picked him up by his throat. Cochran was slammed against a tree, the air immediately expelled from his lungs. Stubbornly refusing to give up, the sheriff began kicking the beast in the stomach. He continued to do this even as the oxygen supply to his brain became more and more depleted. The world began to turn black and as the last moment of his life came to a close, Cochran's eyes drifted up to the forest canopy and the blue sky beyond. A sadness washed over him as he realized he'd never slowed down to appreciate the beautiful things in life.

Darkness…

***

"Please wake up!"

The voice was friendly but clearly panicked. It had a pleading tone but demanding too.

"Sheriff, wake up!"

Cochran's eyes fluttered open and he again gazed upon the sky above him, minus the forest canopy.

"Wh—what happened?" he muttered in a raspy voice, just above a whisper.

"The wood ape got you," the voice replied.

Cochran turned his head to the familiar voice and realized it as Cliff Lowe speaking to him.

"I thought I was dead."

"You should've been."

It was a different voice this time, yet still familiar. This one colder and less sympathetic to his current state. Cochran looked over at the man speaking and blinked his eyes, trying to focus. The blue-rimmed spectacles gave it away.

"When you feel up to it, I think a thank you is in order," Dr. Michael Emmerich said with an arrogance he made no effort to stifle.

The sheriff stared at him, bewildered.

"He showed up just in time and saved your hide," Cliff explained. He then looked over to his right and gestured with his chin for the sheriff to have a look.

Cochran used his hands to push himself up to a seated position on the ground and immediately winced when he felt the pain in his left shoulder.

"Careful, Sheriff," Emmerich said. "Your shoulder appears to be dislocated. There is an ambulance on the way."

With Cliff's help, he finally managed to sit up and his eyes widened when he realized what Cliff was trying to get him to see. To his left, a hulking, hairy mass lay on in the dirt, breathing deeply. The sight startled him to the point he nearly fell over.

Cliff laughed and patted him on his uninjured shoulder. "It's alright, Sheriff," he said soothingly. "It's knocked out. The doctor and his men found you in the woods and popped that thing in the ass with a few tranquilizer darts as you lost consciousness."

Cochran sighed and then attempted to get on his feet. It was a struggle, but with Cliff's help, he finally was standing.

"I suppose you're right," he said, glancing at Emmerich. "I owe you a big thank you. So, thank you."

Doctor Emmerich acknowledged him with the narrowing of his beady eyes but he said nothing.

"But how the hell did you know I was out here?" Cochran asked.

Emmerich shrugged. "I have my ways."

The sheriff, now feeling somewhat rejuvenated, furrowed his brow and approached the doctor. "Bullshit," he snapped. "Tell me how you knew I was out here."

"Perhaps we can discuss that matter later," Emmerich said. "At this time, I think getting you medical attention is more important."

As if on cue, a white ambulance, trimmed in orange and blue, rolled onto the gravel driveway that led to Cliff's home. As the paramedics emerged from the vehicle, Emmerich turned to two other men that, judging by the way they were dressed in all white, were also from the lab and had accompanied him.

"Let's strap the specimen to the backboard and load it into the van," he ordered them.

As the two men went to the task, Cochran approached Emmerich, grabbing him by the arm. "How did you find me?" he persisted.

Doctor Emmerich glanced at the sheriff's hand, now firmly clutching his bicep. He wrenched his arm free. "Oh please," he snapped. "Anyone in this county with a police scanner can find out more than enough information to track your every move, Sheriff."

Cochran opened his mouth to discuss the matter further but before he could, he was swarmed with paramedics.

"I'm fine," he grumbled.

"It's just precautionary, Sheriff," a red-headed woman said as she pulled a latex glove over her hand. "Raise your chin and let me look at your neck."

Cochran looked on as Emmerich's men loaded the wood ape into the back of a white van. His eyes then moved to where the female paramedic was standing. Her arms were crossed, and her lips were pursed slightly. She and her counterpart did not even seem to pay any attention to anything the men in white coveralls were doing. "Sheriff, raise your chin, please."

He sighed and then did what he was told. The woman gently moved her fingers along his throat, prodding slightly. "Does that hurt?"

"No," he lied.

"That's surprising," she muttered. "Anything else hurting?"

Cochran closed his eyes. He knew what was coming next. "Yeah, I think my shoulder is dislocated."

The woman did a double-take and then looked over at her counterpart. "Did you know this?"

The man nodded and drew near them. "Yeah, sorry, forgot to tell you."

The redhead rolled her eyes. "Well, come on then," she told the man. "This is your specialty."

The male paramedic smirked and gently examined Cochran's shoulder. "Sheriff, I'm gonna need you to come over to the ambulance and lay down."

Cochran sighed again and then trudged gloomily over to the ambulance. From that point, he was given instructions on how to lay and what to do with his arm. The next thing he knew, the male paramedic had grabbed his arm and pulled it. Cochran howled in pain and obscenities.

"Sorry about that," the paramedic said, his slight smirk returning. "Most people would rather I just surprise them."

The sheriff wiped tears from his eyes and forced himself to refrain from grabbing the guy by the collar. "Well, I'm not most people, son."

"Does anything else hurt?"

It was the redhead again.

"Absolutely not," he lied again as he slowly moved his shoulder around. Truthfully, he wondered if one of his ribs was cracked.

"It's going to be very sore," she said. "Even worse tomorrow."

"Thanks," Cochran answered as he exited the rear of the ambulance.

"Are you sure you won't come to the hospital so they can look you over a bit more?" she asked.

"Absolutely not," Cochran said, purposely using the same phrase and tone again.

He made his way to his patrol car and as he opened the door to get in, the male paramedic called out to him.

"Hey, Sheriff! Is it true what happened to you?"

Cochran stared at him.

"Was it a Sasquatch that did this to you?"

The sheriff adjusted his hat and bit his lower lip. "What do you think, kid?"

The man looked over at the redhead. She shrugged.

"I think it's probably true," he said finally, grinning.

Cochran nodded and looked toward the trees behind Cliff's home. "Well, if it is, I'd probably get going if I were you."

He then got into the car and backed out of the gravel driveway. As he sped away, the paramedics looked to Cliff Lowe standing behind them with his arms crossed.

"There is definitely more of them out there if you guys want t—"

"No, that's quite alright," the redhead said as she climbed into the passenger side of the ambulance. "I want no part of this."

"Me either," the man said as he got behind the steering wheel. Cliff could see he was staring intensely into the forest. "I figured it was true. I'm glad they caught that thing. Something like that on the loose tonight would've been bad."

CHAPTER 12

Dr. Michael Emmerich sat beside the unconscious creature and marveled at his size. It was by far the largest he'd ever seen and not just in height. He couldn't wait to get the beast back to the laboratory so he could promptly have half of its body shaved. He'd be able to get a good look at the muscle structure and then he'd truly be able to appreciate how powerful the wood ape was. There was barely enough room in the van to contain it and though the wood ape was heavily sedated, he could not help but consider what would happen if it awoke suddenly.

Push that thought aside, he told himself.

"Dr. Emmerich, there are construction signs ahead," the driver called out to him from the front seat.

He positioned himself so he could see out of the windshield and adjusted his blue spectacles. "We don't have a lot of time for delays," he said, a bit perturbed.

The driver glanced over at the passenger beside him as he pulled a map that had been tucked over the sun visor and unfolded it.

"There's an alternate route but it's an old country road that winds through the woods," the man said, glancing over his shoulder at Emmerich.

Emmerich sighed bitterly. "I suppose we have no choice. Time is of the essence. Just get us there as quickly as you can, Mr. Johnson," he told the driver.

Johnson followed the other man's direction and soon the large white van was rumbling along a narrow road enveloped with thick pine trees on either side. The sun was now in the western sky. Emmerich glanced at his watch.

3:12 p.m.

"How much more time is this going to add to our drive?" he asked.

Johnson rocked his head back and forth as he thought and then said, "Probably fifteen minutes…give or take."

Doctor Emmerich wasn't pleased with that answer, but he held his tongue. After all, there was nothing Johnson could do about the situation. As he looked out the windshield, the pulsing light that originated from the bright sunlight piercing through the passing trees made him a bit drowsy. Emmerich soon felt his eyelids getting heavy and as he shook the cobwebs from his head, he caught a glimpse of something that startled him.

Did the wood ape's eye just flutter?

He stared at the creature's face intensely without blinking. He watched for the slightest sign of movement but after a couple of minutes, he saw nothing. There were cabinets lining the upper walls of the van and after brief contemplation, Emmerich arose and opened one containing syringes. As he prepared another tranquilizer, Johnson glanced at the rearview mirror, watching him.

"Everything alright?" he asked.

"Yes, yes, everything is fine," Emmerich said quickly. "Just preparing another dose to make sure he stays heavily sedated since we've added a little bit of time to our journey back."

"Do you need any help?"

"No, I'm quite alright," the doctor replied. "Just keep your eyes on the road, Mr. Johnson."

Johnson shrugged and shook his head.

Emmerich turned the syringe sideways and placed it in his mouth so he'd have use of both his hands. He then reached for and tugged on the leather restraints keeping the wood ape planted solidly on the wooden board it was lying upon. They were still as tight as they possibly could be without constricting the creature's breathing. Satisfied with his inspection, he then retrieved the syringe and prepared to inject the wood ape's arm with more than enough sedative to keep it asleep well beyond the time it would take them to arrive at Walker Laboratory.

The van met a pothole just as he was about to pierce the beast's arm and the jolt was so violent the doctor nearly dropped the syringe. He cursed under his breath, straightened his spectacles, and then promptly—maybe even angrily—pushed the needle hard into the creature's skin. No sooner did he do so, did the wood ape's good eye open wide. Its mouth opened simultaneously, revealing the terrifying rows of sharp, blood-stained teeth. An ominous growl erupted from the opened maw and the realization of what was occurring startled Emmerich to the point he fell backward before even pushing the plunger of the syringe forward.

The doctor opened his mouth to scream a warning to Johnson and the other man up front, but he wasn't quick enough. The wood ape's muscles bulged and the leather straps that had been holding it in place burst free at the buckles. Johnson noticed what was happening and immediately slammed on the brakes, which in turn sent Emmerich hurtling forward. His head struck one of the metal overhead cabinets, momentarily dazing him. The sensation of warm blood trickling down the bridge of his nose jarred him back to reality and the doctor immediately rose to his feet and scrambled to find another syringe.

The wood ape, sensing that it was trapped, drew back its powerful legs and kicked outward against the rear van doors. The doors swung open wildly in response and the sweet scent of the pine forest made its way quickly to the creature's nose. The wood ape then darted from the van just as Emmerich made another attempt to pierce its arm with another tranquilizer dose.

"What do we do?" Johnson screamed frantically. "What do we do?"

"Quiet down!" Emmerich demanded. "Stay calm."

"Where is it?" the man in the passenger seat replied, his head swiveling in all directions.

"It's no longer in the vehicle, and as long as we stay inside, it will not be able to hurt us," Emmerich stated assuredly.

As if on cue, the vehicle lurched slightly, as if something had jarred it from the passenger side.

"What the hell was that?" Johnson asked in a voice just above a whisper.

"We need to go," the other man said. "We need to go now!"

The vehicle was jarred again, this time harder. So much so, Emmerich sensed that the passenger-side tires were momentarily lifted from the ground.

"Mr. Johnson," Emmerich said, as he wiped more blood away from his brow, "I think we should leave now."

Johnson nodded and immediately planted his foot on the accelerator. As soon as he did so, the vehicle was struck again, this time with enough force that it went completely over on its side. Emmerich's head again struck a metal cabinet as he was abruptly hurtled through the air with the force of the impact. This time, the blow knocked him out cold.

"Dr. Emmerich!" Johnson pleaded, still craving direction on what to do. "Dr. Emmerich!"

Emmerich did not respond and the van began to roll. Johnson and the other man screamed in horror as they realized the situation had completely gone beyond their control. The wood ape continued to roll the large van as if it were no more than a wooden barrel. Emmerich's limp body continued to take repeated awkward blow after blow and Johnson could've sworn he heard a bone snap. As the vehicle continued to tumble, the two men managed to keep relatively safe as their fastened seat belts kept them from sustaining any significant injuries. It also managed to keep them aware of their plight and they soon came to realize they were being shoved toward a steep ravine.

"We've got to get out of here!" Johnson yelled as he gripped the steering wheel tightly.

The other man didn't reply, and Johnson wondered if he'd been heard. Or perhaps he was entirely too terrified to talk. Though disoriented, he began to fumble for the button to release his safety belt. It took another roll of the van for him to finally find it, but as soon as he did, he pressed the button. Johnson dropped painfully onto the van ceiling and soon realized his efforts to escape the rolling deathtrap were futile. Wide-eyed, he caught a final glimpse of the steep ravine and the jagged rocks below through the windshield as the wood ape made one final push. Suddenly, the environment became eerily quiet. Johnson realized the van was now in freefall and a mere three seconds later, he met his untimely and rather painful death.

CHAPTER 14

John Milk arrived at Walker Laboratory just before 4 p.m. He'd headed to the facility as soon as he'd been told of the rogue wood ape's capture. It was his hope that he'd arrive just before Emmerich and it appeared he'd done just that.

"Nope, they haven't made it yet," the older man at the guard shack said, glancing at him over a newspaper. "Should be here any minute."

John nodded and went on to park near the entrance of the building. He strolled inside the building and stopped at the front desk where an attractive brunette sat with her nose in a romance novel.

Do any of these folks actually work?

"Ma'am," he said, clearing his throat as he spoke. "May I use the phone?"

The receptionist was momentarily startled and quickly put the book aside. "I'm so sorry," she said sweetly. "I didn't even hear you come in."

He smiled at her. "Must be *some* book."

She chuckled nervously and moved her own desk phone to where he could reach it.

"Thanks," he said as he began to punch the number that would get him a specific room at the Baker County Hospital.

"You have news?" Honeycutt said when she answered.

"How did you know it was me?" he asked.

"Who the hell else would be calling me?"

He leaned on the desk and shook his head with a bit of delight. She was certainly acting more like her old self again. "Yeah, I have news."

"Well, spit it out."

"We caught the rogue."

There was a momentary pause on the other end of the line and through the silence, John could sense Emma's relief.

"Wow, thank God," she muttered finally.

"Yeah, Sheriff Cochran got banged up a little, so we've got him largely to thank."

"So, I'll give him a kiss on the lips when I see him," she said bluntly. "Where's the Squatch at now?"

"In route to Walker Laboratory as we speak," John answered, and he peered out the window to see if there was any sign of the approaching white van. There was not.

"You think Emmerich knows what he's doing?"

John sighed and then bit his lip. "I guess I'll know here shortly," he answered. "I'm actually standing in the lobby of the building waiting on them to arrive."

She let out an exasperated sigh of her own. "You get to have all the fun while I'm stuck in this damn hospital."

"Which is exactly where you need to be," he responded quickly.

"I think I'm going to ask for some crutches and get out of here," she said. "I need to start moving around. I think I could even drive a car."

He stood up straight. It was sometimes difficult to tell when she was serious and when she was speaking in jest. "You keep your ass in that bed," he snapped.

"You're not my father, my lover, or my boss," she growled. "So, don't take that tone with me. If I want to get out of this bed, I damn well will do it."

He rolled his eyes.

Stubborn bitch.

"Fine, do whatever the hell you want to do," he muttered back. "But the rogue is sedated, and Kurt Bledsoe is still locked in a cell at the jail. There is absolutely no good reason for you to press your luck."

There was a long pause where she said nothing, and he could only hear her breathing softly.

"You there?" he asked.

"Yeah, I'm here."

Her voice was firm and a bit icy. John knew he was pushing the envelope.

"I'm just trying to look out for you."

"Yeah," she replied. "I know."

There was a different tone to her words this time. *Regret?*

"I'll try and come visit later," John said, sensing her frustration. "You stay in that bed and I'll bring you some Halloween candy."

"You never told me what you're going to be," she answered him.

He smiled and turned to peer out the huge glass windows that made up the front side of the lobby. He could see a patrol car pulling up to the guard shack and he recognized it as the vehicle belonging to Sheriff Cochran.

"You know, I think I'm gonna go as a federal agent," he said.

There was another pause and he could imagine her rolling her eyes. "Alright, Milk, your poor attempts at humor are my cue to go back to bed."

"Suit yourself," he muttered. "I'll drop by later."

"Thanks for the warning."

John hung up the phone and approached the sliding glass door entrance just as Sheriff Cochran was entering the building. He immediately noticed a sling over his left arm.

"What happened to you?" John asked, looking hard at the sheriff's injured arm.

Cochran shrugged it off. "Another day, another wood ape," he muttered. "Another day in Baker County."

"The rogue did that to you?"

"Yeah, but it was worth it," he answered. "Emmerich showed up just in time."

"Lucky you," John said. He looked beyond Cochran to the long black pavement that connected the parking lot of the Walker Laboratory to the highway beyond. Still no sign of Emmerich's van.

"I'm surprised you beat him here," John said, still staring out the window.

Cochran looked behind him, half-expecting to see the white van coming to a halt just outside the door. Instead, he saw nothing except the quickly setting sun beyond the pine trees. He returned his attention to John.

"You mean Emmerich hasn't made it yet?"

John looked him in the eyes. "No, he hasn't."

Cochran swallowed hard and his face grew ashen. "If he's not here, then something is wrong. They left before me and should've easily beat me here."

"Damnit," John said with disgust. He moved toward Cochran's patrol car and got in as the sheriff jumped in behind the steering wheel. The large car rumbled to life and seconds later, they were on the main highway, siren blaring.

"Any idea where to look?" John asked as he worked his way out of his sports coat and loosened his tie.

"Yeah, I do," Cochran replied, his attention squarely on the pavement ahead of him. "There was some construction going on not far from Cliff's house. The quickest way to Walker Laboratory was a detour down a narrow road that is hardly ever used anymore. It winds through a dense part of the forest where there are no houses or stores for miles."

John leaned over, resting his head on the passenger door window as he watched the trees zip by outside. "I don't understand," he muttered. "If you left after Emmerich and had to take the same detour, it seems to me that you'd have come across him at some point if something went wrong."

Cochran shook his head. "I thought about that," he answered. "There are a lot of deep gulleys off the road and over the years, I've worked a few car accidents that ended in those very spots."

John sat up straight again and looked at him. "Sheriff, if they did have a car accident, I think you and I both know what most likely would've caused it."

Cochran frowned and his eyes stared ahead of him, unblinking. "Yes, and if that thing escaped, we've got big problems."

John sighed but said nothing.

Once they reached the narrow-secluded road, the sheriff slowed their pace significantly.

"Keep your eyes peeled," he said.

Darkness crept in around them and the sun was all but gone. Cochran's mind drifted elsewhere to the town square of Dunn. He knew only minutes from now, the place would be swarming with trick or treaters as they dispersed in all directions to trick or treat the nearby neighborhoods.

"I can't see anything," John said, clearly frustrated.

"It's just getting too dark," the sheriff replied.

He reached over and turned on the spotlight that was attached to the car near the door. As soon as the light flickered alive, it illuminated what appeared to be a man limping along the shoulder of the road far ahead of them.

"Do you see that?" John asked, pointing.

Cochran accelerated in response and as they drew near the man, they both were astonished to find it was Dr. Emmerich. The doctor was limping and collapsed to his knees as the car slid to a stop next to him. John immediately rushed to his aid.

"What the hell happened, Doc?" he asked frantically.

Emmerich's hair was caked with blood and it was evident he'd suffered a head injury. He looked at John, his eyes watery and weary. "You know what happened, Agent Milk," he answered flatly. "The wood ape is loose, and a lot of people are going to be in danger tonight."

CHAPTER 15

They both helped Emmerich to the backseat of the patrol car where he could lie down. He continued to mutter about the dangers the town of Dunn was going to face during the night as they helped him. Cochran agreed with the doctor's chilling words, as did John. However, upon learning the whereabouts of the mangled van, they could not leave without checking to see if the other men had survived the crash as Emmerich had.

"They're here," John called out with despair. He'd climbed into the ravine and was looking up at Cochran above him. "It's too late for them though."

"You're sure?"

John nodded somberly. "Trust me," he said. "They're dead."

The sheriff nodded and offered John a helping hand after he made the difficult climb back to the top.

"Have you got someone you can send over here to get them?" John asked as he dusted his pants off.

Cochran nodded. "My brother-in-law is the county coroner," he answered. "I'll get him and his guys on it."

"Any ideas on how we deal with the wood ape now?"

The sheriff shook his head and began walking back to the patrol car with John in tow. "All my deputies will be out tonight patrolling the town. If it shows up—and I still think it's a big *if*—then we'll be ready to deal with the threat immediately."

They reached the car and after getting inside, John looked back to check on Emmerich.

"How are you holding up?"

The doctor groaned and rubbed at his head. His blue-rimmed glasses were gone, and John wondered just how much he'd be able to see without them. "My head is aching fiercely," he moaned. "But that's not the issue. Sheriff, you and your men must find the wood ape as soon as possible. I fear the creature will be unable to refrain from the temptation that will present itself tonight when the city of Dunn becomes overrun with children."

John looked over at the sheriff. "When we get back to the station, get me a shotgun. I'm going to patrol the area too."

Cochran nodded. "We'd be glad to have the help."

By the time they returned to the Dunn city limits, darkness had fallen, and the streets were beginning to become taken over by multitudes of small ghosts and goblins. Upon their arrival at the station, they helped Emmerich inside and helped him lay down on the couch in the lobby.

"Shelly, call an ambulance for him, will ya?" Cochran said, glancing over at her. "And why are you here? It's late."

Shelly picked up the phone and began dialing numbers. "I didn't think it was a good idea for no one to be at the station while the—umm, Kurt Bledsoe, is still detained and recovering."

"How is he doing?" John asked.

Shelly held up a dismissive finger when someone picked up on the other end of the phone line. She requested an ambulance and gave a brief rundown of what was going on with Emmerich before returning her attention to John. "He's doing quite well," she answered, hanging the phone back up. "He has recovered much faster than I anticipated."

"That's good news," Cochran said while John nodded in agreement.

"How is Agent Honeycutt?" she asked.

John told her and then hurriedly tried to change the direction of the conversation. "Sheriff, what about that shotgun?"

He nodded, disappeared down the wood-paneled hallway, and then quickly returned, tossing him the weapon. John caught it one-handed and then snatched up a box of shells the sheriff had slid across the desk to him.

"Just tell me where I need to go."

"Eastern side of town," Cochran replied. "There's a couple of neighborhoods over there but they are much smaller and not nearly as populated. I don't expect there to be a lot of trick-or-treating going on over there, but it wouldn't hurt to have some eyes there just in case."

"I'm on it," John replied as he headed out the door.

"Hold up," the sheriff called after him.

John paused just as Cochran tossed a radio at him.

"Keep that on and communicate if you see anything. All my guys have been instructed to do the same. If something is reported out, we all head over to that spot to assist."

"Got it," John said, turning away.

Cochran then looked over at Shelly. "Tell you what," he said. "You hang out here for a couple of more hours until the kids start to thin out. At that point, I'll head on back and relieve you."

She smiled and gestured to a crossword puzzle on her desk. "I'm not going anywhere," she muttered.

***

By the time all the deputies, the sheriff, and John reached their respective positions, the streets were filled with costumed children all eager to load up on sweet treats. Cochran was tasked to keep an eye on town square, the area that was undoubtedly the heaviest. The center of downtown Dunn contained a small park named for the town's first-ever mayor, Paul Church.

Every Halloween, Church Park became peppered with local business owners that set up booths and gave out candy. Colorful banners were draped across the front of each booth's table to proudly display the name of each business represented during the event. Almost every child in Baker County, regardless of which neighborhood they lived in, drove to the town square to participate. It was a quick trip to score a lot of candy, thus the vast popularity with all the children and parents.

The sheriff left his patrol car at the station since it was such a short walk to the town square. Upon his arrival, he was met with plenty of friendly smiles from parents and excited waves from children. He smiled and waved back, happy to know that none of them had any idea of the potential danger they were in. A large live oak centered the square and Cochran hurriedly made his way over to it. The space underneath its branches were darkened with shadow. It would provide the perfect place for him to observe his surroundings in all directions.

He leaned against the rough bark and crossed his arms. It was a cool night and if memory served, the local meteorologist on the morning news had mentioned it getting below freezing by midnight. A cup of coffee would've been nice, and he contemplated making his way over to Frank Conner's Wedgeworth Furniture booth where he knew a warm pot would be waiting. Just as he'd made up his mind to stifle the urge for a few more moments, a young girl's scream pierced through the night air. The sheriff immediately bolted toward the direction of the sound and his running transitioned into a brisk walk as he soon realized the ruckus originated from nothing more than a quarrel between a young girl and her older brother. She was dressed as a cowgirl, her brother a pirate, and their mother was giving the young man a stern talking to.

Cochran took a deep breath, relieved that the matter was a trivial one and nothing of concern to him. It was still early, but he quickly found himself wondering how the others were doing. He snatched the walkie talkie from his belt.

"Any news out there? Over."

Static.

"Nothing yet, boss. Over."

It was Billy. He was assigned the Cedar Hill subdivision.

More static.

"Nothing my way either. Anything going on in the town square? Over."

This time, it was John.

"Eh…that's a negative," Cochran answered somewhat sourly. "I suppose it's a good thing. Over."

"Hell yeah, it's a good thing," John replied. "No news is good news tonight. Over."

***

"Ms. Honeycutt, can I get you anything else? My shift is about to end."

The nurse was a pudgy little woman with a beautiful face and smile to match. She had red curly hair and her face was peppered with freckles. She'd just brought Emma a pitcher of fresh ice water to get her through the night.

"No, thank you," Emma answered with a smile of her own.

The nurse wandered over to the window and glanced out. Emma's room was on the third floor of the four-story building. Her room overlooked the town square and Church Park.

"My, my," she said. Though her back was turned, it was evident by her tone that she was still smiling. "Look at all those kids."

"Big turnout, huh?" Emma asked.

"Oh yes," she answered. "Looks like there are a lot of little Ghostbusters out there this year."

Emma chuckled at that and then turned her attention to the television mounted high on the wall. An episode of Moonlighting was playing. She hated that show.

"Well, you have a good night, sweetie, and I'll see you tomorrow," the nurse said as she began to make her way to the door.

"Hey, do you mind turning the television off on your way out?"

"Sure," she replied. "Anything else?"

"Nope, I think I'm all good now," Emma answered.

"If you need help getting to the restroom—"

"I won't," Emma interjected. She glanced over at the crutches that had been brought into the room earlier. "I have to start using those sometime."

"I suppose that's true," the nurse said. "You have a good night, dear."

With the television off, the room became eerily quiet. Emma closed her eyes to try and sleep. She could just barely make out the sound of children's laughter from the park below as she drifted off.

CHAPTER 16

Shelly Snow put down her crossword puzzle to check on Kurt Bledsoe. It had been a while and the last she'd seen of him, he'd been fast asleep. She moved through the heavy metal door that led to the corridor between the jail cells. She stopped at the first one on the right and glanced into the tiny window. To her surprise, the burly creature that Kurt Bledsoe had become was sitting on the floor. It was the first time she'd seen him in any other state than lying down.

"Well, look at you," she whispered.

Kurt snapped his furry head in her direction, his green eyes piercing.

Shelly's jaw dropped open slightly. "Wow, you can hear really well," she said, surprised that he'd heard her whisper on the other side of the door.

Kurt cocked his head sideways and his large eyes narrowed.

"Are you feeling better?" she asked.

Her only answer was a blank stare.

"Are you hungry?"

The large head was still a moment then nodded ever so slowly.

Shelly's brow lifted with excitement. "Oh my gosh, you're intelligent," she said.

Kurt looked at her with sad eyes, seemingly unphased by her compliment.

"Alright," she said. "I'm going to go find you something to eat. Be right back."

Kurt's eyes watched her move out of the window frame and once she was gone, he stood. He began pacing the room, considering options on how he could escape. As he took a hard look at the four concrete walls around him, a momentary feeling of panic took over. He wondered how long he'd be confined to this room. He wondered if they'd be kind enough to set him free. Sheriff Cochran, he knew, was a good man. A man that wouldn't intentionally sit and watch harm come upon anyone. He was, after all, partially responsible for his escape from Walker Laboratory the year before. There would be no escaping that place again if Sheriff Cochran did not make it so.

Kurt's thoughts turned to his sister Marie. He hoped she was doing well and absolutely didn't blame her for getting away from Baker County. She probably believed as everyone else involved did that he'd finally been totally and completely consumed by the monster. Truthfully, he felt himself leaving the creature's body a little more each day. It would not be long before there would be nothing left of Kurt Bledsoe. He wondered how things would transpire after that. At this point in time, it seemed that there were indeed worse things than death. He was living proof.

***

"The crowd has really thinned out over here, over," John said, somewhat relieved, into the radio.

"Well, that's not the case here," Cochran shot back. "Why don't you come on over and join me in the town square, over."

"10-4, on the way, over," John replied.

Cochran glanced at his watch and figured there would be at least another hour of trick or treating before the crowd thinned out in the town square. None of the other deputies had reported anything unusual in their respective areas. The last thing he wanted to do was count his chickens before they hatched, but he began to seriously consider the possibility that the rogue wood ape wanted no part of human activity after some of the difficulties it had experienced throughout the day. The thing was undoubtedly hurt and even fearful.

"Excuse me, Sheriff."

Cochran turned and found an elderly lady that reminded him quite a bit of Aunt Bee from the *Andy Griffith Show*.

"Yes, ma'am?" he asked with a smile.

The short, plump woman sighed and seemed a bit uncomfortable.

"Are you alright?" he asked.

She then smiled at him, though nervously, and her eyes darted around as if she was trying to make sure no one was within earshot before she spoke.

"Sheriff, I just wanted to tell you that I thought I saw something rather odd over behind the fire station," she said, glancing in the direction of a big red fire truck parked outside the station.

He arched a brow. "Oh? What did you see?" he asked.

She shook her head. "Well, it was probably nothing," she muttered. "I mean, it is Halloween, after all."

"What did you see?" he asked again; this time, there was a sternness to his words.

"I suppose it could've been a man in a gorilla costume," she said, her tone clearly one oozing embarrassment.

Cochran's heart rate picked up. "You saw a man in a gorilla costume?"

"Yes, I believe I did," she said with a nervous chuckle. "As I said, I know that's not too incredibly odd considering this is Halloween night but…"

Her words trailed off and her eyes again moved toward the fire station.

"But what?" he asked, urging her on.

"Well," she continued. "It's just, that had to be the tallest man I've ever seen in the entire state of Mississippi."

"How tall?" Cochran asked. Now his own eyes were focused heavily on the vicinity of the fire station.

There was another nervous chuckle.

"Oh gosh," she muttered. "I know this is crazy, but that man had to be at least eight feet tall. It was a fantastic costume from what I could see."

Sheriff Cochran immediately grabbed his firearm and began jogging toward the fire station. Before he'd even realized he'd done it, the sling that had been supporting his left arm had been shed and he was fully using both arms again. He figured the adrenaline now shooting throughout his extremities was numbing any pain that had remained in his shoulder.

"Good evening, Sheriff," a man said, stepping out of the fire station as he approached. It was Sam Kendall, the Dunn fire chief. He was holding a bowl of Halloween candy.

"Evening, Sam," Cochran replied. "You see anyone in a gorilla costume wandering around out here?"

Sam thought about it and then chuckled, his large belly jiggling as he did so. "No, I don't recollect seeing anyone in a gorilla costume tonight," he replied. "I did see a kid dressed as Chewbacca earlier though," he added as an afterthought.

"Thanks," Cochran answered, and he began to move toward the rear of the station. "Do me a favor and stay here," he said to Sam as he disappeared around the corner.

There was little light behind the brick fire station and Cochran immediately took note of the dense foliage and forest just behind the structure. It would've been an easy place for the rogue wood ape to emerge undetected. Cochran was grateful that "Aunt Bee" had noticed it and alerted him to what she'd seen as it seemed no one else—not even Sam—had seen anything.

The sheriff reached for his flashlight and began shining it in all directions. There was no wood ape lurking behind the building, but something else *did* catch his eye. He knelt to the sandy earth and shone his light upon a set of massive footprints, clearly belonging to the wood ape. They appeared to be fresh and clear evidence that "Aunt Bee" hadn't been imagining things. He reached for his radio.

"Agent Milk, what's your 20? Over."

"Be there in about five minutes. What's wrong?"

"It's been spotted," Cochran answered. "I need all deputies to head over to the town square at once. Over."

There was a lot of static and *10-4*s that came back at him. Cochran shoved the radio back onto his belt again turned the beam of his light across the forest edge. He squinted his eyes and peered hard into the foliage, looking for any sign of movement, but found none. There was a moment where he considered venturing into the dense vegetation but realized that would be a bad idea, especially since backup was on the way.

After considering it, Cochran thought it best to hold his position and be as quiet as possible. Perhaps if he got quiet, the beast would be unaware of his presence and emerge from the forest. He turned the light off and found a darkened corner to hide behind on the rear of the fire station. Cochran then crouched low to the ground, turned the volume on his radio all the way down, and for the first time, he felt a hint of pain in his left shoulder. It seemed some of the adrenaline was wearing off. He remained that way for at least five minutes and it then occurred to him that John had probably arrived. He'd have to go retrieve him and fill him in on what's going on.

"Sheriff Cochran...are you back here?"

It was Sam Kendall again.

Cochran shook his head. *Didn't I tell him to stay out front?*

"What's wrong, Sam?" he asked but remained in his darkened enclave.

Sam's head snapped toward the direction he'd been speaking from. Clearly, he was unable to see where the sheriff was hiding. "Nothing is wrong," he answered. "You'd just been gone a while. I was starting to worry."

Cochran took a deep breath and tried not to sound annoyed. "Everything is fine, Sam," he answered. "I'm just checking on something. Do me a favor—look out from for Agent Milk. You're familiar with him?"

"Yeah, I know him and that little firecracker partner of his," Sam replied. "She with him? I thought I heard she was in the hospital."

"She is," Cochran said, shaking his head, again trying not to sound annoyed. "Go find Milk and bring him back here, will ya?"

Sam nodded and turned to look for Milk. As soon as his back was turned, Cochran watched in horror as the rogue wood ape burst from the forest with lightning-fast speed. Before Sam could even comprehend what was happening, the beast grabbed him by the back of the neck and then proceeded to slam his face hard into the brick wall. Sam fell limp to the ground and the wood ape then pounced upon him, biting down onto the back of his shoulder. The creature tore flesh from

Sam's lifeless body and if it knew Cochran was watching, it did not seem to care.

The sheriff quickly rose from his hiding place and proceeded to fire bullets into the wood ape's side as it feasted upon Sam's flesh. The beast snapped its head toward him, glaring at him with rage from it's one good eye. Cochran continued to fire rounds off until he realized the gun was empty.

CHAPTER 17

The wood ape rose from the still body of Sam Kendall, its ugly gaze still planted firmly upon Sheriff Cochran. The sheriff began to frantically reload his gun, though he wasn't sure why. It seemed the bullets he'd fired into the massive creature had done little damage. If anything, it just made the beast even more angry. The rogue wood ape began lumbering toward him, and in a terrifying sort of way, the non-urgency of its movements made him even more fearful. The creature seemed to know how helpless he was in the matter.

Just as he was placing the final bullet into the cylinder on the pistol, the rogue wood ape reached down and snatched the weapon away. It then tossed it into the forest like a frisbee and looked down upon him with a hatred he didn't even know was possible.

"Get on with it, damn you!" he spat furiously. "Finish me off! Just leave those people alone!"

He could hear screaming and other sounds of panic from the square. Most likely, all the children and parents had heard the gunfire and were confused and frightened about what was going on. *This is a good thing*, Cochran thought. While they were undoubtedly making their escape, the rogue wood ape was towering over him, apparently forgetting about their presence. The beast reached down with its massive hand and picked up the sheriff by the collar of his shirt. Cochran could smell the putrid aroma of death coming from its mouth, and he could see the blood and bits of Sam Kendall's flesh covering its fangs. Cochran had been in this position before. He'd gotten lucky before. This time would be different. There was no one coming to save him. He closed his eyes and suddenly felt the sensation of being thrown through the air. He opened his eyes just as his head struck a tree.

Cochran opened his mouth to wail in pain, but no sound came from his lips. His body fell to the damp earth. He tried to get up from the ground, but his body would not respond. Something deep inside him was broken. Whatever that *something* was, it was important enough to shut down his ability to move his extremities. He could only lie there, looking up at the stars above. His breathing had become ragged and difficult. Cochran soon became aware his lungs were filling with blood. This was truly the end for him. Though he could not move, and his breathing was becoming quite labored, his sense of hearing was still operational. The heavy sound of footsteps was approaching, and he knew full well what was coming. He was unable to turn his head, but he was, however, able to shift his eyes to the left. He could see the silhouette of the harbinger of his death looming over him. Cochran then took the deepest breath he could muster and closed his eyes for the final time as the heavy foot belonging to the rogue wood ape slammed down upon his skull, crushing it.

***

"Where is Sheriff Cochran? Have you seen him?" John asked, frantically.

Frightened parents and children ran by him. He found himself in a flood of panicked people, going against the current in his desperate search for the sheriff. Finally, when he realized no one was going to stop to talk to him, he grabbed a woman by the arm, forcing her to stop. The woman looked at him fearfully and he quickly showed her his badge to calm her.

"Tell me what happened," he demanded.

She could see the hardness in his eyes and knew he wasn't going to release her without an answer. "There was gunfire behind the fire station," she said, her voice trembling. "A lot of gunfire!"

John released her and began sprinting toward the fire station. He could see the blue strobes of the deputies' patrol cars arriving behind him, but he did not wait for them. In fact, he didn't stop running at all until he rounded the corner at the rear of the firehouse and found the body of Sam Kendall laying there, bleeding out in the dim light that crept over from the town square lights. He paused to kneel and take the man's pulse. Unbelievably, he was alive.

There was a ruckus in the trees behind him. John already had his weapon drawn and he rose to investigate.

"Sheriff, you out there?" he asked.

Something felt very wrong about the situation. There was a tension he could literally feel in the air. Something horrible had happened. With slow steps, John moved into the foliage toward the direction that he'd heard the movement. He pulled a small flashlight from his pocket to illuminate the path ahead. Seconds later, he was staring upon a gruesome discovery. There was no way to identify him by looking at his face. What had once been his head, was now a bloody, gory mess. It was the uniform and name plate that had given it away. Sheriff Cochran was dead.

John fell to his knees and the tears welled up in his eyes. He'd been too late. The wood ape had killed him. He heard footsteps approaching behind him.

"Guys, don't come down here," he said, doing his best to regain his composure.

"What's wrong?" Billy called out. "Did you find the sheriff?"

"Sheriff Cochran is dead," John said very matter-of-factly. He rose to his feet and walked back toward the rear of the firehouse. Billy saw his face and frowned, fighting back tears.

"You saw him?" he asked.

"I did," John answered, nodding.

Billy attempted to walk past him, but John grabbed his arm. "Billy, don't," he said, almost pleading.

The deputy wrenched his arm free and ignored the request. Seconds later, John could hear him weeping. There were two other deputies now present and they picked up on what had happened.

"Gentlemen, you know as well as I do that the sheriff wouldn't want us sitting around blubbering like a bunch of babies about his death," he said. "That thing is still on the loose and we owe it to the sheriff to protect this town and county."

"I'm going to get a shotgun," one of the men said, turning away.

John followed him. "Good idea."

It was then that the screaming returned.

***

Emma Honeycutt sat straight up the minute she'd heard the gunfire outside. She hobbled over to the window and looked at the town square below. People were frantic. There were screams and panicked families scattering in all directions.

What the hell is going on?

As she was peering outside, the door to her room swung open.

"Ms. Honeycutt, honey, you need to lie down," the nurse said, noticing she was out of bed. "What are you doing?"

"What's going on out there?" Emma asked, still staring out the window.

The nurse walked over beside her and seemed surprised when she saw the commotion outside. "My goodness," she said. "I have no idea."

"I heard gunfire," Emma said, glancing over at the nurse. "Did you hear it?"

She shook her head. "I'm sorry, but I did not. Had no idea anything was happening."

"I've got to go down there," she said, the features on her face hard and determined.

The nurse shook her head. "Honey, there is no need for that, I'm sure the sheriff has it all under control. Why don't you lie back—?"

"Where are my clothes?" Emma asked, glancing down at the hospital gown she was wearing.

"Your partner...Agent Milk," the nurse said, thinking aloud. "He got your clothes to have them laundered. He said he'd bring you some back by."

She sighed and rolled her eyes. "I assume he hasn't yet."

The nurse smiled and shook her head. "Afraid not."

Emma huffed and then hobbled her way over to where he crutches rested against the wall.

"What are you doing?" the nurse asked, sounding a bit frantic.

"I told you," she said, placing the crutches under her arms. "I've got to get down there."

The nurse's mouth dropped open and it was clear she wanted to argue the matter further. After a moment, she simply asked, "If you're going to do this, at least tell me how I can help."

Emma smiled, thankful that the nurse was beginning to relent. "Well," she began a bit sheepishly. "Can I borrow your car?"

CHAPTER 18

John scrambled back into the town square while Billy and the other deputies went after more firepower. He soon discovered that the rogue wood ape had attacked again. There was blood and body parts strewn about through the grassy area between the gazebo and fountain. On the top of the gazebo, appearing like a cross between King Kong and an ugly stone gargoyle, stood the hulking, bloody beast peering in all directions as if he were in search of his next victim.

John scanned his surroundings and could see that, for the most part, the citizens of Baker County had managed to escape. It appeared there had only been one victim and, as terrible as it was, he was thankful to find that it was an adult and not a child. As he'd been watching the wood ape and chaos, John reloaded his firearm and once he'd shoved the magazine home into the grip, he again began to open fire upon the beast.

The wood ape glared at him, an evil sneer cracked its hideous face, and then the beast roared in a fantastic rage that no doubt rattled the windows in all the businesses surrounding the square. The wood ape beat its chest and then leapt from its perch upon the gazebo, its massive feet meeting the earth with a very pronounced *thud*. The wood ape began to tear across the grass, quickly eliminating what had once been roughly a fifty-yard gap between it and John.

John, for his part, continued to fire off rounds, some of which he knew didn't even contact the beast. The bullets that did seemed to do little, if anything, to slow the wood ape's pace. Once the last round was spent, John again frantically went to work at reloading the weapon. He kept one eye on the approaching wood ape and knew there would be no chance in completing the task before the beast tore into him.

The wood ape was mere feet away from him when suddenly a thunderous blast erupted from John's right. This time, something struck the wood ape with enough force to stun the creature. John snapped his head around to find one of the sheriff's deputies ten years away from him, the barrel of a shotgun smoking in his grasp.

"Hell yeah!" John shouted gratefully. He then finished reloading his firearm as the deputy stopped beside him.

John looked at the man's name plate.

T. Rivers

"Thanks, Deputy Rivers," he said. "I owe you one, my friend."

Rivers nodded but kept his eyes on the wood ape moving slightly on the ground near them.

"We'll talk about that when that thing is dead," he answered.

"Hit him again," John commanded. There was a pain in his gut, a lingering side effect of his still coming to terms with the death of Sheriff Cochran.

"With pleasure," Rivers answered, and he pulled the trigger.

The weapon thundered again, but to John's utter horror, the wood ape suddenly rolled out of the way with a quickness he did not expect. Again, the creature was on its feet again.

"Shit," John whispered. "Run!"

He turned in retreat, but Rivers did not, opting to instead fire the gun yet again. The wood ape dodged the assault once again and then it was on Rivers. John could only look on with terror as the beast tore its fangs into River's throat. Blood sprayed from the wound as the beast tore flesh and cartilage from Rivers' neck. The deputy was dead before he hit the ground.

"Damnit!" John screamed in anger. He began firing rounds again and soon, he was joined by Billy, the deputy who began unloading every shotgun slug he had available into the direction of the lumbering wood ape.

"This isn't working," Billy said, his tone a mixture of anger and hopelessness.

John again ran out of ammunition about the same time Billy did. The wood ape had taken on more lead but it still advanced toward them, though somewhat slower now. John tossed his gun aside, realizing it would not do him any more good. He looked around for a place they could hide to give him some time to think. He looked to his right and saw a row of historic buildings aligned tightly together. Two of the buildings had a very narrow opening between them.

"Follow me," he said, and then he took off in a dead sprint toward the opening.

He could hear Billy following, and beyond him, the sound of the wood ape's massive feet stomping the ground as it gave chase. John's heart was beating with such intensity he feared it would burst. He refused to look back as he ran though he could *feel* the creature closing in behind him. With no time left to spare, John contorted his body in a fashion that allowed him to slip through the opening with ease. He turned just as Billy made it to the opening as well, but to John's horror, the deputy was ripped backward, the shotgun falling from his grasp.

John could hear Billy scream as his body was hurtled through the air like a rag doll. He was unable to see where the deputy landed and decided it probably wouldn't matter much anyway. Billy would most likely be dead, but John knew if he had any chance, he'd better pick up the shotgun. As he picked the weapon up from the ground, the rogue wood ape threw its muscled, hairy arm into the small opening. John jerked back and narrowly missed being snatched up by the beast's violent grasp.

"Please help us."

The voice was feminine and tiny. John looked over his shoulder and found a young girl standing in front of three other children. "Don't let it hurt us, please."

John looked at the wood ape's arm as it continued to flail and thrash wildly, its black claws scraping at nothing in desperation.

"Cover your ears, kids," John said as he picked up the shotgun. Three seconds later, he fired right into the wood ape's open palm.

John watched as the projectile tore through the beast's hand. It yelped in paid and jerked it's arm back. He smiled as he realized for the first time, he'd witnessed the creature definitely feeling pain. The wood ape jogged away, yelping in agony as it did so. Satisfied that they were at least momentarily safe, John began to venture further along the narrow alley between the two buildings. He soon came to realize that the opening widened more and more until finally he reached the rear of the buildings. It was only a matter of time, he knew, before the wood ape figured out how to get behind the buildings to attack them again. John again looked at the kids. He forced a smile and knelt before the girl.

"What's your name?" he asked softly.

She was dressed as a cowgirl. Her hair was braided into two pigtails. "Vanessa," the girl answered back.

"That's a beautiful name," he replied, marveling at how incredibly calm she was. "Who are these other two young men?" he then asked, glancing at the two boys behind her.

One kid was dressed like a vampire, the other a pirate.

"I don't know them," the girl said, turning to look at the boys. "We just all ended up here when that monster started hurting people."

John took a deep breath and nodded. "How old are you, Vanessa?"

"Eight."

"And do you know where your parents are?"

She shook her head and for the first time, he could see a tiny bit of emotion welling up.

"Don't you worry," John said, doing his best to stifle the girl from crying. "I'm gonna find your parents and get you out of here real shortly." He then glanced to the boys. "That goes for you two also."

The boys nodded and Vanessa smiled. She took a deep breath and put on a brave face.

"That's better," John said, giving each of them a moment more to regain their composure.

He then grabbed the radio from his belt.

"Shelly, this is Agent Milk, do you copy?"

There was a pause, then static. Finally, "I hear you, Agent Milk. Is everything okay?"

John closed his eyes as he imagined how terrible the news of Cochran's death would be on Shelly. And if that wasn't enough, the deaths of the deputies also.

"Things could be better," he replied. "We've got a real situation out here and I'm afraid we are fighting a losing battle. Have you checked on Kurt Bledsoe lately?"

"Yes, I have," she answered. "He's doing much better and is getting up and moving around."

John sighed and held the radio a moment as he contemplated the decision he was about to make. There were few options and he wasn't even sure if the crazy idea that had just formed in his mind would even work.

"Shelly, I need you to listen to me very carefully," he said. "I want you to lock down every door in that station except the front door. I want you to open the front door wide and prop it open."

"Agent Milk, are you trying to send that monster in here on me?" she asked nervously.

John smiled and shook his head. "No, ma'am, not at all. Once you get the front door open, I want you to open Kurt Bledsoe's cell. When he's freed, I want him funneled out the front door so he will have to enter the town square."

There was a long pause and then more static.

"Agent Milk, are you suggesting what I think you're suggesting?"

"Yeah, I am," he answered. "I told you we're fighting a losing battle and we need some help."

"But the last time those two fought, it didn't end well for Kurt," she shot back.

"Look, Shelly, we don't have a lot of time here," John quipped, a bit harshly. "People are dying out here and frankly, I'm out of options. Turn him loose, please."

There was another long pause.

"Alright," she replied softly. "I'm going to let him out. Over."

"Thanks, Shelly...over."

CHAPTER 19

Once Shelly Snow had locked down all the doors except the front one, she quickly made her way back to the cell where Kurt Bledsoe had been locked up for quite some time. She was out of breath by the time she reached it and forced herself to calm down a bit before she spoke. It was clear from Agent Milk's tone that things outside had gotten very bad. The mere suggestion of releasing Kurt Bledsoe spoke to just how terrible it must've been. Once her breathing had finally slowed enough to speak calmly, Shelly leaned near the tiny window and peeked in.

Kurt Bledsoe was pacing the room and it was almost as if he'd sensed something was wrong too. He immediately noticed her presence and stopped moving at once. He turned his large brown head to look at her, his green eyes shimmering.

"We need your help," Shelly said to him. "That monster that hurt you is back and now it's hurting the good people of this county."

Kurt took a breath through his nostrils and his eyes narrowed.

"I've been asked to set you free," she said. "I don't even know if we let you go if you'll even try to stop that thing. I certainly wouldn't blame you if you didn't."

Kurt continued to stare at her intensely.

"But if you're willing to help us, we'll be grateful," she said.

She reached down and began to turn the key that would in turn open the heavy door. She paused and took one final fierce glance at him.

"When I open this door, please don't eat me," she said a bit nervously.

Shelly closed her eyes and released the locking mechanism. She then hurriedly stepped back. Once she was clear, a few seconds ticked by and then suddenly the door flailed open and Kurt Bledsoe darted from the cell without even giving her a second glance. Shelly reached for her radio.

"Agent Milk...he's free."

***

The rogue wood ape had fled the alley where it had been shot in the hand for the cool waters found in the town square fountain. It was there that John had spotted it as he ushered the three children he'd recovered into the lobby of the post office where several others had sought refuge. After giving strict orders to stay inside with the door barricaded, he ventured back into the town square again, the barrel of the shotgun leading the way.

The rogue wood ape did not see him as its back was turned while it tended to its wound at the fountain. John's heart raced, but as he knew there was no way to be sure if Kurt Bledsoe would assist, he felt the opportunity before him could not be passed by. Each step he took was careful and quiet. John even took slow control breaths. It was well known how well the wood apes of Baker County could hear and smell, but it was his hope that the creature was so involved in nursing its hand that it would not notice him. He got within thirty feet of the beast when it suddenly raised its head and sniffed the air.

Oh shit…

The rogue wood ape turned its body and released a deafening roar of fury that turned John's legs to gelatin. He instinctively pulled the trigger on the shotgun but this time, the wood ape was more than ready. It moved with the quickness John had become all too familiar with and then charged at him. The creature barreled into him like a freight train and the force of the impact sent him hurtling backward through the air and onto the hood of a car. The windshield behind him shattered when his shoulder crashed into it and he immediately felt something inside him break. What it was, he had no idea.

The wood ape began walking toward him slowly and John could see a menacing smile on its wicked lips. The beast had seemingly forgotten all about its injured hand even as the wound continued to trickle blood onto the ground beside it. John was unable to move his legs, but he could, however, move his left arm. He began reaching for his firearm only to cruelly find it was no longer there. It was then he remembered tossing the useless weapon aside. The wood ape was only an arm's length away from him when it suddenly stopped and sniffed the cool night air. John looked on as the creature's terrifying features shifted away from arrogance to one of concern.

Out of seemingly nowhere, the yowl of another wood ape erupted throughout the night sky. John could hear a sound of something approaching and it almost sounded like the gallop of a horse. He turned his head just in time to see the form of Kurt Bledsoe sprinting across the town square with a burst of furious speed. The rogue wood ape had little time to react as Kurt leapt high into the air and crashed down upon him with a force that made the ground shake. Unable to move, John could only lay where he was and watch in unbridled fascination as the two beasts became entrenched in a spectacular fight.

Kurt had momentarily pinned the rogue to the ground. Straddled over him, he then placed both of his large hands around the beast's throat and began to squeeze the life from him. The rogue struggled for several seconds but then abruptly pulled its knee hard into Kurt's back. He yelped in pain and momentarily lost his grip around the rogue's throat. The rogue wood ape then punched Kurt hard into the chest, sending him flying backward and into a phone booth, crushing it in the process.

Kurt brushed the glass from his shoulders and then returned to his feet, again charging at the rogue. The rogue charged back at him and the two creatures clashed together so hard, the sound reminded John of a car crash. The two beasts fell to the earth and then rolled several times over it. The clawing and gnashing of teeth sent hair and blood flying through the air. John wished there was something he could do to help but he was completely immobilized.

The fight continued until the two beasts reached the fountain and, to his relief, John looked on as Kurt managed to force the rogue wood ape's head beneath the water to try and drown him. The rogue thrashed and clawed at Kurt, cutting deep gashes in his chest as it did so. With its efforts appearing to be futile, the rogue changed its strategy and instead pulled Kurt into the fountain with him. The move surprised Kurt and he tumbled forward, suddenly finding himself now being held underwater.

With the rogue seeming to now have the advantage, John quickly became concerned that Kurt was on the verge of drowning. He began to yell and scream at the rogue, doing anything he could to draw its attention and give Kurt a moment of opportunity. The rogue completely ignored him and continued to push down with the full brunt of its weight on top of Kurt. A shotgun blast suddenly tore through the night and into the back of the rogue. It howled in pain and snapped its head around to find another deputy pointing the weapon at him.

John was pleased to see one of the remaining deputies jump back into the fight at the last second, but as the rogue wood ape glared at him with intense anger, he suddenly realized the man's life was in the balance.

"Run!" John yelled.

The determined deputy rose the barrel of the shotgun to fire again, but before he realized what was happening, the rogue had jerked Kurt from the water and hurled him through the air. Kurt landed on the deputy, crushing him in the process. John watched as Kurt coughed up water and glanced regretfully at the deceased deputy lying before him. He then rose to his feet and charged at the rogue once more. The two beasts were again enthralled in a battle, resulting in more clawing and biting.

John heard Kurt howl in pain multiple times, and it started to become apparent that the smaller creature was beginning to tire. The rogue wood ape soon had him pinned to the ground and began to pummel him with blow after blow. Kurt thrust a fist upward into the rogue's stomach, momentarily pushing the wind from his lungs. This time, it was Kurt on top and he began to give back the punishment he'd just taken himself. Blow after blow was dealt upon the rogue wood ape's face and John could feel the tide of the battle beginning to take a turn. Blood began to pour from the rogue's nose and mouth and its one good eye was all but swollen shut.

"Finish him off!" John screamed as he noticed Kurt beginning to slack off the assault.

Kurt's punches slowed until he finally stopped altogether.

"What are you doing?" John asked, desperately wanting him to finish the job.

Kurt rose to his feet and looked down at the pitiful mess the rogue wood ape had become. He then looked over at John. Their eyes met.

"You can't do it?" John asked, astonished.

Kurt's green eyes softened, and he shook his head once. He then began to approach John, seemingly sympathetic to his injured state.

"No," John yelled. "Don't come over here. You should leave before Walker Laboratory or someone else shows up that will want to take you away."

Kurt stared at him and there was a sadness in his expression. It reminded John that the beast standing in front of him had once been a teenage boy. He couldn't imagine how helpless he must've thought being trapped inside a body that did not belong to him.

"Seriously," he urged. "You should go! I—this town—we'll never be able to repay you for what you've done. The least I can do is set you free."

Kurt looked beyond the buildings to the forest behind them.

"That's right," John said. "Get out of here!"

Kurt looked back at him and allowed a slight nod. His eyes were watery and if John didn't know better, he was on the verge of tears. He looked to the trees and back to John again as if he were struggling with the decision.

"There's nothing to think about here…go!"

Kurt turned and took a step forward but was abruptly struck across the chest with a black iron spike. To John's horror, the rogue wood ape had gotten up and pulled a metal spike from the fencing that surrounded the flagpole near the center of the square. Kurt stumbled on his feet, momentarily dazed by the blow. He spun slightly, facing John, a worried expression on his face. Their eyes met and then the tip of the black spike burst through Kurt's chest as the rogue wood ape impaled him from behind.

"No!" John screamed.

Kurt collapsed to his knees and then onto his side, his breathing labored and ragged. Blood poured from the wound. The rogue stood over him and beat its chest victoriously. With Kurt finally incapacitated, the creature turned its attention back to John. It seemed as if the beast knew he was ultimately responsible for Kurt's involvement and he moved toward him with a sinister sneer. John looked around him, frantic to find something—anything—he could use to defend himself.

As the rogue wood ape strode closer to him, the eerie sound of a revved-up car engine rang out and John turned his head in time to see a white station wagon speeding across the town square. The car tore through flowers, fencing, and shrubbery before finally crashing hard into the rogue wood ape. The car continued its trajectory until it crashed through the front of a nearby grocery store.

John craned his neck around as far as he could to see what was going on. The door to the car swung open and Emma clumsily fell out. She pulled a set of crutches from the car and after a bit of work, managed to get onto her feet.

"Honeycutt!" John yelled. "Get away from there!"

He looked on as she seemingly ignored him and carefully made her way through the debris to check on the status of the wood ape.

"Don't worry," she said. "He's dead."

She turned and began hobbling over to him.

"Are you alright?" she asked.

John sighed and shook his head. "No, I'm not." As he said the words, pain began to radiate from his toes all the way up to the space between his shoulder blades. "Something's wrong. I can't move my legs."

When Emma finally reached his side, she grabbed the radio on his belt and called the police station.

"Shelly's got help on the way," she said, dropping the radio clumsily on the hood.

"Are you okay?" he asked her.

"I'm fine," she said. "Just a little lightheaded. Took a lot of work to get down here and save your ass."

He chuckled at that. "Well, I owe you one, that's for damn sure."

"Yeah, you do," she said and then she glanced over at Kurt. "I'm going to go check on him."

"Be careful," John warned.

She drew near Kurt and was surprised to see he was still alive. His eyes glanced over at her. They were soft and distant.

"Thank you," she said, plopping down beside him. "Now go and be free."

Kurt opened his mouth slightly and then stared up at the stars above. Moments later, he was gone, finally free of his prison.

CHAPTER 20

"Agent Milk, can you hear me?"

John blinked his eyes a few times and waited for the world to come into focus.

"Cold? Is that you?" he asked wearily.

"Yes, it's me, Agent," Cold replied.

John kept blinking until finally the chiseled features of Cornelius Cold came into full view.

"I—I thought you were looking into that island in the Bermuda Triangle…the one with the dinosaurs."

Cold smiled nervously. "Agent Milk, there are a few civilians in the room," he said. "Careful with what you say."

John nodded. As he surveyed his surroundings, he soon realized he was in a hospital bed.

"Am I…paralyzed?" he asked, forcing the words out of his mouth.

There was a chuckle beside him originating from another man. John turned his head and found a doctor standing on the opposite side of his bed from Mr. Cold.

"No, sir, you're not paralyzed," he said flatly. "You did, however, suffer a bit of nerve damage when a couple of the lower vertebrae in your back became fractured. This is affecting the feeling in your legs but the surgery we performed—"

"Wait," John interrupted. "Surgery?"

"Yes," Cold answered, amused. "You just came out of surgery this morning. They must've given you some really good drugs."

John took a deep breath and closed his eyes. "I'd say so," he muttered, trying not to sound embarrassed. "How is Agent Honeycutt?"

"She's resting in the adjacent room," Cold said. "She reaggravated her leg injury with her automobile heroics. Needless to say, she too just came out of surgery."

"If it wasn't for her, I'd be dead," John replied.

Cold nodded and glanced over at the doctor.

"Doc, would you mind giving us a moment?"

The doctor smiled and nodded. "Of course not," he said. "I've got my rounds to make. I'll check back on your later, Mr. Milk."

John shook hands with the doctor and moments later, he and Cold were alone.

"I'd say you owe some of the reason you're still alive to the bigfoot specimen you released," Cold said, his tone suggesting a bit of disappointment.

John looked away as he was unwilling to let Cold see his reaction.

"I did what I felt I had to do," he replied firmly.

Cold nodded and placed his hands in his pants pockets. He was dressed in his usual black suit and black tie. "Of course you did," he said, his tone turning a bit friendlier now. "I put you and Agent Honeycutt in charge here for a good reason. I trust your decision. It's just unfortunate that the specimen was lost in the process. There will probably never be another Kurt Bledsoe ever again."

John shrugged. "I suppose that's true," he said. "But would that be a bad thing? He'd become a tortured soul. A textbook case of wrong place, wrong time."

"You're referring to the meteor that made him what he became?"

"Of course that's what I'm referring to," John answered. "He was just a kid with his whole life ahead of him, and he had to be at the exact right place at the exact right time for the circumstances that made him what he was to occur. It's a tragic situation, and I hope you're right. I don't want to see that happen to anyone else ever again."

Cold huffed. It seemed to John he had different thoughts on the matter but elected to keep them to himself.

"So, what became of the rogue?" John asked, trying to change the subject. "I'm sure our guys at Walker Lab are cutting him into a million pieces as we speak so they can study him. Am I right?"

Cold looked down at the floor and his mouth became a straight line.

"What?" John asked, sensing he was about to get some bad news.

Cold looked back up and directly into his eyes. "The rogue got away."

John's eyes widened and he shook his head. "That's not possible. It was dead," he answered.

Cold shook his head back. "No, Agent Honeycutt *thought* it was dead, but it most certainly was not. By the time our folks got over there to retrieve the body, it was gone."

John suddenly felt sick to his stomach. His mind immediately went to little Lucas Hurst, Sam Kendall, the sheriff's deputies, and of course Sheriff Cochran. They'd all lost their lives to the beast. Would their deaths ever be avenged?

"That's not what I wanted to hear," John said sourly. "I'm going to hunt it down when I get out of here. There's a guy at the edge of town, his name is Cliff Low—"

"No, you're going to let it go, Agent," Cold cut in.

John was taken aback. "Excuse me, sir?"

"We've spent a year of your and Agent Honeycutt's time trying to locate Kurt Bledsoe. With him now out of the picture, the two of you will be reassigned to a new location."

John glared at him, unable to hide his displeasure. "Sir, I think that's a terrible mistake," he said. "If we leave, then the rogue will continue to kill."

"Not your problem," Cold shot back.

John swallowed hard and fought to keep his composure. "Sir, with all due respect, this department specializes in studying the paranormal. What is more paranormal than a county full of these creatures? One of which has gone rogue and developed a taste for human flesh."

Cold gave him a hard look. "Agent Milk, the presence of those creatures is why Walker Laboratory exists here. Again, not your problem. You and Agent Honeycutt will be reassigned and that is final."

"Well, at least tell me they're going to catch it," John said, almost pleadingly.

Cold shrugged. "I'm not at liberty to say."

John's mouth dropped open. "Oh, come on, sir," he groaned. "Don't shoot that company jargon at me. After everything that's happened, I feel I have a right to know."

"You're not going to like the answer."

"Try me."

"Fine," Cold said, somewhat exasperated. "I don't think there are any immediate plans to capture the beast. What they want to do instead is try and study it from afar."

John stared at him in disbelief. "*Study it?*"

Cold nodded. "We know where the creature's den is located and it's not far from an old antebellum home in a secluded portion of the county. The thing's been spotted there on more than one occasion hunting deer and other wildlife. We're wondering if it would be bold enough to go after a human there."

"Well, I can answer that," John said. "Yes, it would most certainly would be."

Cold smiled. "I thought so."

John suddenly felt a sick feeling in the pit of his stomach. "Wait a minute," he said. "You're not actually telling me that we're going to stand by and *observe* what this thing does. We're not going to actually watch it kill a human being and do nothing."

"If it'll help us understand how it hunts...how it kills," Cold said. "Then yes, that's exactly what I'm telling you."

John stared at him again with disgust. "Sir, I can't be a part of that."

"And you won't be," Cold said. "That's why I'm reassigning you."

"What about everything that happened in the town square?" John asked. "The whole damn county practically witnessed what occurred. Lives were lost!"

"Yes, and those families will be compensated handsomely," Cold answered. "The citizens of this county will be on board with what we're trying to do."

"How can you possibly know that?"

"Because," Cold said, sounding a bit agitated now. "If they do not, they will disappear. And besides, we've made it clear to each of them that we have a plan in place to keep them safe from the rogue moving forward."

"By basically putting human bait in the antebellum home you mentioned?" John asked, shocked.

Cold nodded.

"This department never ceases to amaze me," John said.

"Moving forward, we will be involved in picking the local law enforcement to ensure what we're trying to accomplish suffers little to no setbacks."

"This is crazy," John muttered.

"Crazy?" Cold shot back. "This is nothing. Crazy is dinosaurs in the Bermuda Triangle."

***

Clifford Lowe walked quietly through the cold forest and found a good spot to wait. Ever since he was visited by special agents dressed in black—he assumed they were colleagues of Agents Milk and Honeycutt—he couldn't shake the desire to go out and see if the rogue was still alive for himself. The agents that had visited him made in a roundabout way threatened him if he ever spoke of what had happened and what he'd seen. Cliff said what he had to say to get the agents to leave, but truthfully, now more than ever, he knew he had to keep watching the beast.

So now he found himself in the woods, waiting to see the creature again for himself. He'd continue to watch, and he'd learn everything he could about the creature's biology and habits until he finally got the opportunity to kill it. It was now his life's work, he decided, to see to it that the rogue wood ape died and paid for what it had done to so many good people in Baker County. He'd see the task through, or he'd die trying.

The End

CHECK OUT OTHER GREAT CRYPTID NOVELS

SWAMP MONSTER MASSACRE
by Hunter Shea

The swamp belongs to them. Humans are only prey. Deep in the overgrown swamps of Florida, where humans rarely dare to enter, lives a race of creatures long thought to be only the stuff of legend. They walk upright but are stronger, taller and more brutal than any man. And when a small boat of tourists, held captive by a fleeing criminal, accidentally kills one of the swamp dwellers' young, the creatures are filled with a terrifyingly human emotion—a merciless lust for vengeance that will paint the trees red with blood.

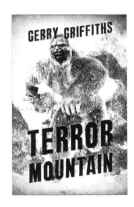

TERROR MOUNTAIN
by Gerry Griffiths

When Marcus Pike inherits his grandfather's farm and moves his family out to the country, he has no idea there's an unholy terror running rampant about the mountainous farming community. Sheriff Avery Anderson has seen the heinous carnage and the mutilated bodies. He's also seen the giant footprints left in the snow—Bigfoot tracks. Meanwhile, Cole Wagner, and his wife, Kate, are prospecting their gold claim farther up the valley, unaware of the impending dangers lurking in the woods as an early winter storm sets in. Soon the snowy countryside will run red with blood on TERROR MOUNTAIN.

CHECK OUT OTHER GREAT BIGFOOT NOVELS

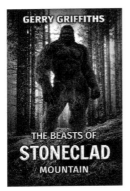

THE BEASTS OF STONECLAD MOUNTAIN
by Gerry Griffiths

Clay Morgan is overjoyed when he is offered a place to live in a remote wilderness at the base of a notorious mountain. Locals say there are Bigfoot living high up in the dense mountainous forest. Clay is skeptic at first and thinks it's nothing more than tall tales.

But soon Clay becomes a believer when giant creatures invade his new home and snatch his baby boy, Casey.

Now, Clay and his wife, Mia, must rescue their son with the help of Clay's uncle and his dog, a journey up the foreboding mountain that will take them into an unimaginable world...straight into hell!

BIGFOOT AWAKENED
by Alex Laybourne

A weekend away with friends was supposed to be fun. One last chance for Jamie to blow off some steam before she leaves for college, but when the group make a wrong turn, fun is the last thing they find.

From the moment they pass through a small rural town they are being hunted by whatever abominations live in the woods.

Yet, as the beasts attack and the truth is revealed, they learn that despite everything, man still remains the most terrifying evil of them all.

Printed in Great Britain
by Amazon